DEVON
GHOST TALES

T0346942

DEVON
GHOST TALES

JANET DOWLING

ILLUSTRATED BY VICKY JOCHER

The
History
Press

*To Jeff Ridge, my long-suffering partner in life, who came with me
to most of the ghost story sites, listened to me while I tried to piece
together the jigsaws of bits of story, and who sat by my side when
the sun went down and I was too scared to write the stories in a
room by myself. He supports me unquestioningly in all that I do,
and I am very grateful for that.*

First published 2018

The History Press
The Mill, Brimscombe Port
Stroud, Gloucestershire, gl5 2qg
www.thehistorypress.co.uk

© Janet Dowling, 2018
Illustrated by Vicky Jocher

British Library Cataloguing in Publication Data.
A catalogue record for this book is available from the British Library.

isbn 978 0 7509 8545 1

Typesetting and origination by The History Press
Printed in Great Britain by TJ International Ltd, Padstow, Cornwall

CONTENTS

INTRODUCTION

When I expressed interest in researching and collecting stories for *Devon Ghost Tales*, one thing was said to me, time and again. *Do we need another Devon ghost story book? Surely there are plenty on the bookshelves already?* And I would agree with you! There are a lot, ranging from Devon-wide ghost stories to localised collections. But, very interestingly, not all of them are ghost *stories*.

Theo Brown, the Devon folklorist, said that 'real ghosts (that is, the kind that someone claims to have seen, heard or smelt) seldom, if ever, have a story attached to them'. Some of these books are gazetteers of reports of ghostly sightings with no backstory, and a few of them are stories telling the backstory. And the former outweigh the latter by ten to one.

So, how to create a balance, be faithful to the story (where there is a story) but also create something new that is not dismissed as 'just another Devon ghost story book'?

Well, I can promise you that I have tried to be thorough in my research. I began by reading every single Devon ghost story book that I could get my hands on, collated the stories and then cross-referenced them. It became obvious which ones were 'collected' from the same earlier sources because they used the same phrases and language. It was also interesting to see how motifs were repeated over the stories; for example, I had three different stories from different places which included a ghost being required to empty out water from a pond by use of a sieve, and each finding that they had to put something in it that stopped the water flowing away.

With well over 200 stories or sightings to choose from, I was aware of Ruth St Leger-Gordon's comment about the story of 'Childe the Hunter'. 'This,' she says, 'is perhaps the best known of all the Dartmoor tales. For this reason, although frequently quoted, it cannot be well omitted here.' I understood the sentiment, and could have easily chosen the more popular ones to include. But that would be just like all the other ghost story books.

At the end of the day, I am a storyteller. Like historians and folklorists, I do the local research and find out what people have said and recorded. The historians and folklorists go on to publish the stories as told to them, in the context of the day the story was collected. However, as a storyteller I stand back, and look at the story from a wider perspective. Who could the ghost be? What are they doing here? Why would they be doing that now? What would be the consequence? Would anyone else be involved? What are the wider human questions that arise from this story? Are there variants of the story that give a different point of view? Thus as a storyteller, a different kind of story emerges!

I whittled it down to sixty that interested me. I made site visits, explored the local area, ferreted in churches, libraries and museums for information and anywhere else that would give me a lead. I even spoke to people at random on the local streets. The main selection process depended on whether I was inspired to write a story when I got home and how much of the local detail I could incorporate into the story.

Some of the stories are my version of ones that have been retold many times; they reflect the detail in earlier writings, what is told locally, and have a storyteller spin to it. Some of the stories are based on a small paragraph of 70–100 words that I found in an old book or magazine article. And some were just told to me in good faith. My research may not have turned up another version of the story, but it has provided some interesting background and context which have inspired the writing. Thus, not just another Devon ghost story book!

Many thanks to Vicki Jocher, Fiona Pickford, Maxine Akehurst, Richard Akehurst and members of Exeter Steampunk for coming with me while I explored the sites. Many thanks to members of staff and volunteers in libraries, museums, churches and the big houses I visited, and in particular to Jannette Fernandez, Jackson and Jo Bruce-Hall, John Tarling and Douglas Hull, who helped me source some of the stories which were not recorded elsewhere.

Many thanks to Jane Corry's writers' group, and Cindy Loo Turner and Marion Leeper (from Sky Possums) for giving me feedback while I was developing the stories. Many thanks to the ninety-five members of the Devon Ghost Tales Facebook page who allowed me to debate some of the dilemmas I was having with research, writing, and even the placing of commas! Many thanks to Adam Golding, Emma Donovan, Caroline Strickland, Marion Leeper, Fiona Pickford, Kathy Wallis and Karen Wilson for reading my penultimate drafts and finding the miscreant commas, bad tenses and other mayhem I created with the English language. Many thanks to Vicki Jocher for her wonderful linocut illustrations. And not forgetting Jeff Ridge, who, among all the other things to be grateful for, also drew the map.

And thank you, dear reader, for choosing *Devon Ghost Tales*.

1

THE RAG DOLL: THE PROSPECT INN, EXETER

The Prospect Inn is on the quay in Exeter next to some craft shops and does a nice line in food and drink. But Christmas Eve holds a dark secret. Sometimes, and only sometimes, a girl in Victorian dress can be seen climbing the stairs at the top of the house. She carries a rag doll in her arms. As she reaches the top of the stairs, she turns, holds the doll to her face and gives a smile to whoever sees her.

*She turns and then is gone, into the attic door. Who is she? We may
not know: all that we do know is that the Prospect Inn used to be
called the Fountain Inn and it was established by Richard Sercombe.*

Richard Sercombe was rightly proud of himself. From the turn
of the nineteenth century he had been the ferryman across the
Exeter quay. Day in, day out. Meeting the same people and total
strangers. He was well known and knew everybody. You wanted
to make a connection, you asked the ferry boat man. They didn't
always know his name but his face was widely known. And if the
odd coin or two made it into his pocket for the little indiscre-
tions that he overheard and passed on, well, all to the good.

His house was on the quayside and his wife Elizabeth would
provide refreshments for the thirsty travellers as they waited for
the ferry. Only a few minutes back and forth on the boat, but
the travellers were willing to take their turn and rest awhile. The
ale that Elizabeth brewed and the simple fare she cooked made
their house a popular stop.

They had only one child to care for: a granddaughter, Betty.
Her father was Elizabeth and Richard's only son, Thomas, but
he had been impressed to serve in the navy and died at sea. The
child's mother had abandoned her in favour of another suitor
and in their grief, the Sercombes took the child in. Elizabeth
had made a rag doll out of the clothes that were left behind by
her son. She used buttons for eyes and cross stitched a smiling
mouth. When she finished the doll, she held it to her nose and
caught the last aromas of her boy, before she called Betty and
gave it to her. Betty swooped it up in her arms and sat on the
stairs at the top of the house, singing and telling stories to it.

Betty had her own role to play in the business. She would skip up to the travellers with the rag doll in her hand and offer to sing them a song, or do a little dance. Amid laughter and good-hearted banter, she twirled and gave her heart out. A coin or several would be tossed in her direction and she would run to her grandmother, who carefully put the coin in her apron pocket. As the night grew later, she would soon give her farewells, walking up the stairs, with her doll dragging behind her, waving to the men below.

Between the three of them, they were industrious and in time Richard was able to buy the house next to his own and convert the two into a much bigger house. Elizabeth's eyes sparkled with excitement at the promise of expanding the business.

As they lay on the paillasses in the new house, Richard said to his wife, 'This will improve our prospects and raise us up. Our granddaughter will have opportunities that we never had. It will be a fountain of good fortune for us. A new future.'

They decided to call their alehouse the Fountain, and hoped that good fortune would surely come their way.

Elizabeth proved to be a clever businesswoman and the alehouse thrived. She brewed more of her own and also bought in ale from the brewery. She and her husband were able to build the business so that eventually Richard hired someone else to run the ferry. The young man, John, took lodging with the family and also helped out with moving barrels and other tasks within the alehouse.

Betty blossomed into a fine young woman. Working in the Fountain, she was a joy to her grandparents as she encouraged the singing and dancing that brought the young men into the alehouse to eat, drink and party. There was many a buck who fancied his chances with her. Not only was she very fair, but they looked around them and saw the opportunity that might come from marrying the sole heiress to a very successful business.

'Dance for us!' they would cry out, and she would jump up on one of the empty barrels and step dance until it rumbled and even toppled over. There was laughter as each man tried to catch her as she fell. But she was nimble on her feet and she gave her favours to no one.

John watched. As the ferry man and erstwhile bar hand, he had seen her grow up and loved her with a passion. He grew jealous each time she smiled at a customer and wanted to lash out when one would put his arm around her waist. She was oblivious to his interest in her. But it was his intention to have her.

He tried to court her, suggesting that they go for walks along the quayside. Anything to have some time with her away from the pub. But she shook her head, smiled at him and always promised tomorrow.

Unfortunately, a promise of tomorrow is sometimes taken as a commitment for today and John had it fixed in his head that they were betrothed. He began to watch her obsessively, marking every smile, turn of her ankle or trill of laughter as a sign she was cuckolding him. Richard was too busy with the business to notice anything, but Elizabeth knew that something was wrong. She tried to caution Betty, warn her against playing with the passions of the men around her. But Betty dismissed the thought from her head. As far as she was concerned, she had grown up with John around and he was nothing more than a friendly, if possessive, uncle. Elizabeth persisted and it was arranged that Betty would go to north Devon to stay with her aunt. The pub was quieter when she was gone and the punters bemoaned her loss but Elizabeth told them how well Betty was faring, living with her family. They gave her a toast and then turned back to their tankards and drank another pint.

Three weeks later John disappeared from his post. Richard was furious but Elizabeth was relieved. Maybe now he was free from his infatuation with Betty. Then news came from north Devon. John had followed Betty there and given vent to his passion for her. She had fought him back and in the process had grabbed a kitchen knife and stabbed him. She was held in the town prison, awaiting trial for murder. Richard and Elizabeth closed the pub and went north to see what they could do. Within weeks it was evident that Betty was bearing a child, forced on her by John. She was released from confinement and returned back to the Fountain.

With her belly growing, there was no dancing, no twirling. Betty kept out of sight of any of the punters, shamed by what her body was doing to her. Elizabeth apologised many times for sending her away, and Richard castigated himself for not seeing what was obvious to others.

Business in the pub continued; there was still plenty of trade.

A storm rolled around the skies the night that Betty gave birth to her child. She was in great pain and the midwives were delayed. Elizabeth did the best she could but by the time the child was born, Betty had given up the ghost.

Elizabeth and Richard were devastated. They had lost their son so long ago and now their granddaughter too. If it was not for the mewling scrap in their arms, who knows what they might have done. Richard could not own up to his feelings of despair and anger. He worked on through the day and the night, putting all his energy into the running of the Fountain. His laughter echoed around the bar, hiding the sorrow that he felt. When the last man had gone from the pub, he would descend into the cellars, kick at the barrels and call Betty's name. Sometimes he would challenge himself to lift the heaviest barrels, hoping the pain in his arms and chest would drown out the grief. But nothing really worked for him.

Elizabeth existed in a fog, barely able to function. She lay in her bed, unable even to rise. Richard would sit by her side and try to give her soup to sustain her. One of the serving women suggested moving the baby into the bedroom. The cot was brought in, alongside her bed. One of the women did her best to feed the child with bread and milk but the little infant sobbed and pushed their hands away. For a long time Elizabeth took no notice of the child. The doctors feared that both Elizabeth and the baby might fade away. Then one night, Elizabeth was tossing in her bed. Richard did not know what to do. Was she asleep or was she awake? Then Elizabeth called out, 'Betty! Betty my love, forgive me.' She sat bolt upright in her bed and then berated her husband for having no light in the room. She swung her legs over the edge of the bed and rose unsteadily. It had been some weeks since she had been out of her bed. Richard was trying to light the lamp, his fingers stumbling over what should have been an easy task.

'The child. Where is the child?' Elizabeth started to move around the room, balancing herself by the edge of the head-board, the bedpost and the sideboard. She reached the cot and stood over the child. Richard wondered if she was possessed. Would she harm the baby?

'Let me hold her,' she said. 'Betty told me to hold the child.'

Richard wrapped the baby in a blanket then held her in front of Elizabeth. Tentatively she reached out, taking the baby in her arms. She pulled back the cloth from around the face. The child opened its eyes and looked up.

'She has your eyes,' said Richard.

'She has Betty's eyes, and Thomas's too.'

Elizabeth turned to Richard. 'I'm sorry. All these weeks. I don't know where I was. I thought I was with them both. Betty and Thomas. But they said I couldn't stay. I had to come back for this little one.'

She looked down at the baby. Then very gently she placed a kiss on the forehead.

'She is our future now,' she said. 'All this is for her now. No matter her father, it's our son and granddaughter that count!'

From that day, Elizabeth was inseparable from the baby. They called her Bess, carrying the name down the generations. Elizabeth took out her sewing things. Among Betty's toys was the rag doll that had been made so long ago. Elizabeth had a fancy that she could still smell her son. Now, from the clothes that Betty had worn, she fashioned a new dress for the doll.

'This material comes from the robe your mother wore at her first communion. And this was the one she loved to dance in. It swirled and twirled behind her.'

Bess was the spitting image of her mother and had the same laughter and eagerness to dance and sing. But Elizabeth kept a close eye on her. She did not want a repeat of the incidents that happened with Betty. So during the day the child would stay close to Elizabeth's skirts, and when the bar became busy she was sent up to her bed.

It became a ritual that she would start up the stairs, hold up her rag doll, kiss it, then turn away to go through the door to the upper room where she slept. Those of the men who remembered her mother would give a loud cheer and the child would have a smile on her lips.

And so life went on. Elizabeth and Richard ran the pub, knowing that every penny that came over the bar would secure a future for Bess.

It was Christmas Eve 1823, and Bess was seven years old. Gales had been wreaking havoc and many travellers were packed into the bar. Even Bess was allowed to help out as there were so many people. But soon she started to complain of earache and

pain when she was swallowing. Elizabeth checked her forehead and found she had a raging temperature.

'To bed, my girl,' said Elizabeth. 'Go up now and I'll come later to see you.'

Bess stood on her tiptoes and reached up to kiss her. Elizabeth wrinkled her nose at the foul breath and pushed her aside.

'Later, my dear.'

Bess turned away, disappointed. She reached for her rag doll. Her body was aching and she found it difficult to put one leg in front of another. She walked very slowly up the stairs, reached the door, then turned and looked down. She kissed her doll and then pushed open the door.

It was a very busy night. Even with the serving women and the cellarman, they were rushed off their feet. It was the early morning before Elizabeth thought about going to bed. She gave a sudden thought to Bess but her own bones were aching and she thought the child would be asleep, so best not to wake her.

In the morning she was surprised to awaken and find that Bess had not slipped into her bed in the night as she usually did on cold mornings. Richard still slept by her side, snoring as usual. She pulled a shawl around her shoulders and made her way up the stairs to Bess's room. It was cold when she entered. Unusually, she could not hear anything. Nothing at all. Just a cooing of pigeons and the seagulls calling outside.

She could see Bess with her bedclothes thrown off her, her rag doll tucked under her arm but still fast asleep.

Elizabeth started to pull the blanket over Bess and her hand just brushed the child's face.

It was cold. Stone cold.

Elizabeth looked again.

Bess was not breathing.

Elizabeth took hold of her shoulder and tried to shake the girl awake.

No reaction.

'Wake up. Wake up!' she screamed.

No reply.

In desperation she pulled the blankets off the child and drew her into her arms. Bess was stiff and unresponsive.

Elizabeth wailed.

The *Exeter Flying Post* of 1823 reports that:

> *Elizabeth Sercombe committed suicide. She went to the salmon pool just beyond the quay, took off her bonnet, shawl, shoes and stockings, and drowned herself.*
>
> *Richard died four weeks later. He was in the cellars throwing barrels in rage, then burst a blood vessel and died.*
>
> *The next Christmas Eve there were reports of a small girl carrying a rag doll, who could be seen going up the stairs, turning round to watch the company and then disappearing.*
>
> *The barmen reported that, when unattended, the cellars would echo with the sounds of the barrels being thrown or misplaced. But no one ever saw who was responsible. Was it Richard?*
>
> *The current publican has never seen a ghost but he felt unnerved when he realised that his child sat on the steps leading up to the attic, to play with her invisible friend – just as the child of the previous publican had done.*

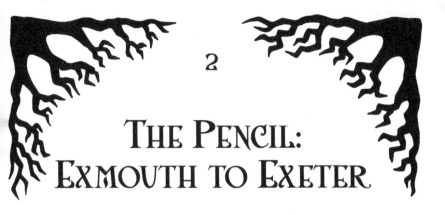

THE PENCIL: EXMOUTH TO EXETER

2

Freddie Carmichael was celebrating the end of year at Oxford University with his friends. They had a few drinks, shall we say, and as they were making their way back to their rooms, they crossed the quadrangle, where stood the statue of the founder of the college.

Freddie was very merry and when he heard a woman's voice in his ear, saying 'Climb the statue!', he did not question why a woman should be in an Oxford college in this year of 1847.

He had not a second thought and scrambled up the pedestal on to its august frame. The outstretched arm was too great a temptation so he positioned himself to swing on to the arm and hang from it, to the cheers of his friends. Sadly the arm, which had survived many such pranks, could do so no longer and with a large CRACK! Freddie found himself on the ground, surrounded by the astonished faces of his friends, and the college night custodians running across the ground.

Thus it was that Freddie found himself in the master's house the next day. He was suitably contrite (if a little hungover) but the master was having none of it.

'You have talent, my lad, but no commitment. Without any purpose in your life you have no direction. Go home today, instead of next week. Take time to discover your passion and decide whether you wish to resume your studies to become the best you can be, or whether you are wasting your time here.'

When Freddie got to Exeter station he took a carriage to return him to the parental home in Exmouth, complete with his trunks of clothes and books. Now to ponder what he would do with his time. Perhaps a lawyer? Perhaps a writer? Never a doctor, though – he was too squeamish with blood.

His mother greeted him affectionately, but his father was aloof. It was always that way and he expected nothing less from either of them. Women were sentimental, while men were strong, held their thoughts to themselves and never expressed an emotion. He knew he would be like his father, but first there was fun.

He left his bags in his room and strolled down to the quayside where the ferry crossed over to Starcross. As a boy, it had been one of his pleasures to ride back and forth, imagining himself to be on the far seas. A child's game, but sometimes in his dreams he remembered the freedom he had imagined. Hughes was the old man who had run it – was he still there? Freddie peered at the boat, trying to make out who was running the ferry, but it was at the far side, at Starcross. It ran from dawn to dusk, but he couldn't wait now for it to return. Tomorrow perhaps he would find out, but tonight was the home-cooked pies of Tilly, the family cook.

It was after dinner that his father summoned him to his office.

'Well, my boy. What is all this then? Sent down early? And the master's not sent a good report!'

Freddie had no excuses to make. He knew he was scraping through, but he thought he was doing well enough. After all, there was plenty of time. There was always time.

But his father had different ideas. 'If you are not going to improve, my lad, then no more university for you. You'll come back home and work for me in the family firm. Either that or you can support yourself. Time waits for no man and you are running out of time!'

Freddie was shocked. His father hadn't spoken to him like this before. His cheeks burned and he pursed his lips as his father stormed out of the room.

He awoke about one o'clock in the morning. Were his father's words still ringing in his ears, or had he overindulged with Tilly's pie? Something had disturbed him. He put his hand to his stomach, but no rumblings were there. He turned on his side in the bed and pulled his blanket about him. That's when he heard the voice again. A woman's voice.

'Go to the ferry.'

It was such a ridiculous thing to hear that he shook his head. Surely his mind was just making up words to fit the creaking sounds of the old house. He turned to the other side of the bed.

'Go to the ferry. The boatman waits.'

21

How strange. The only ferry was the one from Starcross and that had finished at dusk. It wouldn't be working now. He must be dreaming, influenced by his early evening adventure and maybe some of Tilly's cheese. It was a hot summer evening and yet it was quite cool in the room. As he lay there, a shiver passed through him.

'Go to the ferry. The boatman waits. We are running out of time. Do it now.'

Freddie sat bolt upright, and watched as his breath turned white. His skin seemed to be receding from him as if a nail was being drawn over the ridges of his head. Beads of sweat slid down his forehead. He shivered. This was not right. He pinched himself and yelped at the pain he caused himself. He was not dreaming. How could there be a summons to the ferry?

The moon was bright, so he had no need for a light as he swung himself out of bed and pulled on his trousers and frock coat. He laughed at himself for being a fool, easily spooked, but it didn't stop him making his way down the stairs. At Oxford anything like this would be a prank and he would laugh it off, but there was no one else in the house besides himself, his parents and the servants. He opened the front door. Cold air greeted him. Now there was a mist, so that even the moon and stars were blunted in their shining.

Even though the way was obscured, he had spent his childhood in these streets and he found his way to the quay. He could hear the water lapping again at the dock and then a second sound, as if there was a boat moored up.

'Hello?' he called out.

'Ah, there you are! I've been waiting nigh on an hour for you! Come on aboard.'

It was the old boatman, Hughes.

'Hughes, old fellow. Good to see you are still working. But what are you doing here?' asked Freddie.

'Oh! It's you, young sir,' replied Hughes. 'I'd heard you were back from college. I was about to go in for the night, when I heard a voice say, "Take the ferry to Exmouth." I couldn't see anyone, but it was already so misty I thought maybe there was a small boat taking messages that had hailed me. I brought her back here, but there was no one about. Well, I thought, I'm awake now, let's see what happens.'

Let's see what happens, indeed, thought Freddie.

He stepped on to the ferry and Hughes took him across the water. It must have been about two o'clock as he took a step off at Starcross, wondering what to do next. Then he heard, 'Exeter.'

He couldn't work out if it was the same voice or something else. He turned to ask Hughes if he also heard, but the older man had already moored up and was heading for his bed.

'Exeter.'

There it was again. Whatever game this was, he might as well play it out.

Exeter was still a distance to walk and he realised that the atmospheric railway station was very close. He reasoned that it would be quicker to wait and get the train into Exeter than to start walking. Whatever was driving him onwards would want him there in good time. There were some packing crates on the platform, so he settled himself to rest. He woke up as the early morning pick-up train had just made its way into the station. The stationmaster was surprised to see anyone quite so posh up this early, but was more than happy to sell him a ticket. There was no first-class carriage available and he had to sit in third class with all the servants and working men making their way into Exeter to work for the day. He overheard two workmen lamenting that their workmate was up before the assizes for murder and there was no-one to clear his name, even though he said he was innocent. Freddie idly thought that all men declared themselves innocent regardless of their culpability. He pushed himself in the corner of the carriage and tried to catch some sleep.

He woke when the guard poked his shoulder and asked him to leave. The carriage was cleared. His first thought was for his wallet, but it was secure in his trousers.

There were no words in his ear to guide him as he walked the streets of Exeter. Shops and hotels were beginning to open up. Freddie laughed at his fool's errand. He'd been deluded by his own fantasy and now all the impetus had run out. He decided to return home, to get some decent sleep, but the smell of some kippers caught his attention and his stomach persuaded him that breakfast might be a good idea. The kipper trail led him to a small hotel that was most happy to provide him breakfast, but, they told him, he must be aware that they had a full house as many people had come to the assizes hearings. Always a popular sport to see who got off, who was imprisoned and who got the death sentence.

The serving staff were keen to tell him of a case that had caught everyone's interest, as it was a local carpenter. Freddie wondered if it was the same man he had heard the workmen talking about, but thought no more of it until he was making his way to get a carriage back to Exmouth. He passed the assizes house, to see queues of people outside. His interest sparked, he joined them.

There had been a murder of a local dignitary and there was a trail that led to the carpenter. No one else was implicated and the prosecution affirmed that the man was surely guilty. He would be hanged, and rightly so. The carpenter had denied it, of course. But as Freddie listened, he began to realise that the evidence was mainly circumstantial. He hoped the lawyer who was defending the man would point this out.

This was going to be interesting. He sat back in his seat and fumbled in his pocket for his notebook. It might be worthwhile making a few notes while he was observing the case. He took a pencil out of his pocket and wrote down the date and where he was.

The prosecution evidence was now finished and the defence gave the carpenter his turn to speak.

'I know you all think that I did it,' began the man in the dock. 'But I tell you I would hurt no man. All this evidence may point to me, but you know the time when this man was murdered. And I tell you now, on my mother's life (bless her soul), that I did not do it.

'I was working at a house some ten miles away. The owner had asked me to measure up for some shelves and cupboards in the library. It was a long job and the man left me to get on with it. He went into town. There was no key to lock the front door and no servants around, so I thought it best to remain there until the owner returned. There was a knock at the door and I answered it, thinking it was the gentlemen returning. But it was another young man who wanted to consult a book and assured me that the owner was expecting him. He was the gentleman who did see me and who did talk with me at the chiming of the clock, so he would know the hour and can say that I could not have been at the murder. I pray God that that man would only come forward to speak for me, but I know neither his name nor how to find him.'

The courtroom laughed at what passed for his defence. His defending counsel hushed the court to ask a question.

'And why would such a gentleman, in such a library, want to speak to you and to remember you?'

'To borrow my pencil, so that he might write in his notebook.'

The laughter rose again and this time the judge could be seen to smile. His fingers were switching and playing with a cloth on the desk in front of him.

But as Freddie heard those words, something at the back of his mind began to turn and try to worm its way to consciousness. He could feel it working up the ridges of his skull as he tried to grab at it. Something important. Something about a carpenter's pencil. He was sweating with the mental exertion, knowing now that a man's life was in the balance.

And there it was. A memory of a winter's day, barely six months ago, when he had ridden to his friend's house, only to find that the friend had gone out. He had waited in the library, where a carpenter was busy making measurements for a bookcase. He found the book he was interested in and rummaged in his pockets to make a note. His pencil was missing and he had indeed asked the carpenter if he had a pencil he could borrow.

Freddie looked at his hands. Here was the very notebook. He turned the pages to the date in question. There was an entry, written in the distinctive thick lead of a carpenter's pencil. He looked again at the carpenter and realised that the thin drawn face he saw before him now was the more robust fellow he had met six months previously.

The laughter was abating in the court.

Freddie stood up. The judge looked over to him. Silence fell in the court.

'Your honour,' he said, 'I do not understand the path of how I came to be here but here I am. In my hand I hold a dated notebook and on the day that concerns this court, there is an entry. And that entry is indeed written in a carpenter's pencil. It appears that I am that gentleman and I confirm every word this man says. He was with me at the time you have claimed the murder to have happened.'

There was uproar in the court. Freddie was escorted to the judge's rooms where he explained all to the prosecutor and defender. The notebook was displayed, examined and checked for mischief, but in the end upheld by the judge as indisputable proof.

The carpenter walked free.

Outside the court, cap in hand, he found Freddie and thanked him profusely.

'No one believed me, sir. No one. I had no one on my side. All I could do was pray to my dead old mother that she might be able to help me and she found you, sir. She found you.'

Frederick Carmichael nodded. He didn't know what it was that had woken him or guided him to the assizes, but now he knew that there was more to justice than the finding of guilt – there was defending the innocent. He had also learned that time was of the essence after all. He had found his passion.

3

A FATHER'S SINS: PRINCESSHAY, EXETER

I sat in the Chinese restaurant, checking my watch. My cousin John was an hour late. Again. Our fathers were brothers; they had been close all their lives and I supposed I kept in touch with John to respect my dad's memory. I hadn't planned to be at the same university as him, but that's the way it worked out. So I spent my time putting up with him. I ordered some prawn crackers and munched my way through them, my mouth getting drier by the moment. The prawn toast looked good on an adjacent diner's table, so I asked for some of that too.

Finally he arrived. He came into the restaurant, scanned the room for me, paused, looked over his shoulder, shook his head and then spotted me frantically waving at him. He slid into the booth and on to the padded bench opposite.

I was shocked. He was gaunt and thin. I'd known him all my life and he had never been this dishevelled. 'What's happening?' I asked.

He looked at me over the rims of his glasses. It was something he tried to cultivate when we were students, as though he knew a lot more than he was saying.

'Too much.'

Frankly, I'd had enough. I hadn't seen him for ages, then he rings me up out of the blue, demands we meet, then pulls the old being late trick. I guess it suited his ego to think he could attract his cousin's curiosity, but I was beginning to lose patience. I had other work to do and he was keeping me from it.

'Well,' I said, 'I'll order now and when I've finished eating, I'll have to leave. You've got until then to tell me what's going on and that's all.'

Tough love, I suppose my mother would have called it. Sometimes you have to draw a boundary even with family. I knew that John could take outrageous liberties.

'I'm not sure what's going on. But I have to let someone know, just in case.'

He looked at me again. I smiled. This was another of his tricks. Melodrama. Exaggerate a small thing out of all proportion to get attention. I needed to be decisive, otherwise we could be here all night. I waved at the waiter and gave him my order. John declined to eat.

'I couldn't,' he muttered.

'All right,' I said, 'Say your piece.'

'It all started,' he said, 'at the Yule Ball in December. I parked my car in the Princesshay car park and then cut through the shops to get to the Phoenix Arts Centre. It must have been about nine o'clock and the streets were pretty deserted. You remember – it was a pirate theme?'

I nodded. I remembered the evening well. I'd worn a fairly risqué Annie Bonney outfit and then fell over my boots and twisted my ankle. I'd spent most of the evening at A&E, putting up with their curious looks and unvoiced questions.

He continued. 'I stopped at the department store on the corner. They have big windows and the light was good there. I was looking at my reflection, just to check that everything was right. I wanted to make an impression at the ball. Then I noticed that there was someone behind me. It was a woman with a small child. She was just walking past, in the direction of the Art Centre.

'Her dress was long and she wore a cloak over her shoulders. It covered her head so I couldn't see her face properly. She was holding the child's hand very tight. From what she was wearing, I thought she was probably going to the ball too, but I wondered about the child. I made up a story in my head that her babysitter had let her down and she was determined to go to the ball!

'I called out to her reflection "Hey Cinders!" and turned around. But she wasn't there. No one was there. I tell you that there was no way she could have walked away from me and disappeared. I ran up the street. But she definitely wasn't there.'

John was beginning to sweat a bit.

'So she was a ghost,' I said, trying to speed things up. My barbeque ribs had arrived and I was determined to enjoy them. Anyway, my comment was a joke. John is an astrophysicist at the university. Ghosts are definitely not on his radar. He describes them as a natural phenomenon that we have not learned to measure, yet. But he was hesitating.

'And so?' I prompted.

'And so I went to the ball and had a really good time. You've seen the pictures on social media?'

I nodded again. I knew that they'd enjoyed themselves while I was hobbling around the hospital rooms, all by myself.

'But the next day, I couldn't get it out of my mind. Where had she gone? So I thought I'd go back at the same time and under similar conditions to work out where she could have gone.'

Only John would treat a ghost hunt with scientific precision. Not that I thought it was a ghost, but it was an answer I could happily be flippant with.

The duck chop suey arrived, with the prawn chow mein. I waved to John to continue as I tucked in.

'I was in the same car park and then made my way to the department store. I stood in front of the same window and seemed to be there for some time, but it must have been just a couple of minutes. I felt a bit stupid and started gurning at myself.'

The thought of John gurning made me laugh. I had to put down my chopsticks and put my hand over my mouth. He was oblivious to my amusement.

'It can't have been very long when I saw her. And the child. They appeared from Southernhay and then down Bedford Street. They were just walking. She wasn't in a hurry. So I watched what they did, reflected in the window. They went straight past me and then, when they got to that circle of red tiles, in the middle of the square, they just disappeared.'

His voice was quivering and his hand was shaking. He reached out for the jug and poured himself some water. Then he took the table napkin and wiped his hand where he had spilt some. 'I didn't know what to make of it. I walked over to the circle and stood there.

'"Who are you?" I said to myself. And then I heard some laughter. But it wasn't a child, it was deeper than that.'

He paused. 'You know I don't believe in ghosts. However, I *do* believe in energy traces that exist in a space but we can't measure them yet. With a high emotional charge, they could be triggered to stay in one place. We don't have the technology yet, but our brains can pick it up and just make up a story.'

'Go on,' I said. I was getting interested.

'I decided that before I went back again, I would do some research. Was this a phenomenon that other people had experienced?'

I laughed. 'Exeter is full of ghosts! You could be tripping over them all the time.'

'Well, I went on to the internet and you're right. Lots of potential energy sources to be investigated.' He paused. 'You know that the Princess Hay shopping centre was built on the site of the old Bedford Circus? There were some old Georgian buildings that were damaged in the Second World War. Rather than try to repair them, they were demolished. You can still see some of the old houses on Southernhay.'

'So,' I said, trying to work out where he was going with this, 'you think your lady is a historical energy source looking for her Georgian house that has been knocked down?'

He gave me a look that was designed to make me want to crawl under the table.

'No, she was dressed much older than that. I think the energy source comes from the old Bedford House. It was constructed in Elizabethan times and had most of the land that the shopping centre is built on and more.'

'So she's a Tudor ghost – sorry – energy source?'

He gave me a pained look again.

'What's a highly charged emotional event that happened around here in history?' he asked.

I shrugged.

'The Civil War,' he said, as if to a reluctant student. 'Exeter was Royalist, but the Parliamentarians kept trying to take it. Everyone was on tenterhooks, frightened to reveal on which side they stood. There was more than one siege.

'But what is interesting is that Charles I's wife, Henrietta Maria, came here in 1644, because it was a Royalist stronghold. It's where she gave birth to her ninth child. Can you imagine that? The emotions that must have been around at the time. Would Charles win the Civil War? Would Henrietta survive childbirth in such a stressed state? Would the town be taken and they would all be at risk? And what of the new child?'

He looked away over his shoulder, his words just fading slightly. He looked back at me again.

'The queen planned to escape to France, but Cromwell set his fleet at Torbay to prevent that, so she fled to Falmouth in Cornwall. Just weeks after the birth her husband sent her to France to raise support for him. She had to leave her newborn daughter with friends. She didn't see her for another two years. By then her husband was beheaded. I'm not a woman. But imagine leaving behind your child and losing your loved one in such a cruel way!'

I had nothing to say. They were harsh times. I looked at the clock and knew I needed to leave soon. John just went quiet and looked down at the placemat in front of him. I let him have his silence, while I wiped my hands and face on the lemon-scented towel brought by the waiter.

'So, what are you doing now?' I eventually asked.

'I was just thinking. The queen lost someone very important to her, her husband and the father of her child, and was separated from her newborn babe by the actions of Cromwell. That surely must have created a highly charged emotional state. I've been experimenting with a device to measure them. It's a bit primitive, but it's all I've got. And I need someone to help me.'

I laughed again. 'Help you? Why?'

John looked down. 'Because I'm afraid.'

I didn't laugh. For John to come out with that, something must be wrong.

'Tell me,' I said in my best supportive voice.

'I've been back four times now. On my third visit, I looked into the windows and saw her passing. I waved. She stopped and turned towards me. The small child was still holding her hand, pulling her away. She turned back and then they were gone.

'The next time I was there, I set up two cameras to record what was going on behind me. One was an ordinary camera, the other was infrared. I borrowed them from the university. Astrophysics goes over most people's heads, so there were no questions asked why I requested the equipment. I stood in the usual place, waiting for her. They appeared. I waved. She stopped. She turned and took one step towards me. The child pulled her hand again. She was so close. The cloak had fallen back a little and I could see her face in the window. So sad. Oh so sad. Then the child pulled her again and she was gone. I checked the cameras, but nothing was there on either of them.

'I went back home and tried to sleep, planning what to try next. But I couldn't get the look on her face out of my head.

She was so fearful and so downcast. I felt something like a black ball grow in me. First of all it was small and smooth, then it got bigger, felt sticky and was almost bursting out of me. I began to question everything that I did, that I owned, that I had done. I felt a massive failure. I spent the next few days in my room, not wanting to talk with anyone, not eating.'

I remembered a few weeks ago, John had seemed to drop off the social scene. It sounded like he was depressed.

'John,' I said, 'is now the right time to continue with this energy experiment? Perhaps come back to it later?'

'No, you don't understand. The next time I returned, her reflection was already in the window. She was waiting for me. She turned. She took one step towards me. Then another. She was almost in touching distance. I think she's trying to communicate. She has an awareness of me, as I am aware of her. But when I went back home, that black ball was so large inside me, it was in my arms and my legs. I collapsed onto the bed. I didn't move. I couldn't do anything. I'm ashamed to say, I soiled myself.'

He stopped talking. There were tears in his eyes. I leant over the table and stretched out my hand to reach his, but he pulled away from me.

'I shouldn't be like this. I'm an astrophysicist. This doesn't happen to me.'

'Leave it for the time being,' I whispered. I was beginning to worry about his state of mental health.

'I can't. All she has to do is take that extra step and then she can touch me. And when she does that, I'll be wired up to measure any change in my galvanic skin resistance. Primitive, I know, but it might just be the start of a whole new science.'

The alarm on my phone went off.

'John, I'm sorry. I have to leave now. Promise me something, you won't do anything silly.'

'So, you can't help me?'

'Yes, I will, but not tonight. Let's meet tomorrow noon at the Italian lunch place. You can tell me what you want me to do.'

I summoned the waiter and asked for the bill. John remained in the other seat. His face looked even thinner than at the start of the evening and I could see him gripping the edge of the table as he tried hard to hold his hands still. He said nothing, but kept staring down at the empty plates.

'John. Will you be all right? Promise me that we'll meet for lunch and you can show me what you need.'

He looked up at me and gave a smile. He placed one of his hands on mine – so dry – and squeezed it.

'I'll be fine. Thanks so much for listening to me. It has helped. Lunch will be good, and I'll pay.'

I bent down and just gave him the smallest of hugs. I could feel him pull away – he never liked touching.

'See you tomorrow,' I called as I left the restaurant.

I arrived at the Italian place on time and waited for about five minutes before I gave in and ordered myself a Caesar salad. After half an hour it was obvious John wasn't coming. I tried ringing his phone, but no answer. I remembered what he had said about locking himself away and thought about going around to his flat. I was checking my phone for his address, when a news alert from the local paper flashed up. I read it and went cold. My stomach heaved and I felt the room swirl around me.

Local man found dead. John Cromwell, 25, an astrophysicist at the university, was found collapsed in Princesshay in the early hours of the morning, surrounded by electrical equipment. He was rushed to hospital but was dead on arrival. Police are investigating but say it is not a suspicious death.

Did John find his ghost queen? Did she reach out for him and he grasped her hand? Was the excitement all too much for him and his heart failed?

Or was it something more sinister?

Cousins we are, and we share the same surname. We often laughed about it and wondered if we were related to *the* Cromwell. Is that the kind of thing a ghost knows? Did she take his life as a punishment for the traumas of her family all those years ago?

I will never know the answers. But now I never walk through the shopping centre at night. Just in case.

4

THIS FOUL PRIEST: LAPFORD

I t was 1170. Henry II, King of England, was in Anjou, France. He slammed his hands on the wooden table, lifted them slightly and with one gesture swept the papers onto the floor. The parchment that he had been reading, complete with its great seal, fell close to the fire. His goblet of wine crashed to the floor, the red ambrosia seeping across the floor. The plate left on the table rattled to a stop.

The man on whom he had come to depend, who literally fought as his right-hand man, his chancellor, was now the main irritant in his attempts to rule. Henry had been great friends with Thomas Becket, who had been raised to the rank of Archbishop of Canterbury, the second most powerful position after the king himself. He thought he had the authority and support to implement the laws he wanted to rule his lands bountifully. Everything was in place!

But that's when Thomas Becket developed a religious conscience about the role of the Church. He challenged the king at every step of his attempt to establish the rule of law between Church and state. What was the point of all these years of planning, to be foiled at the last moment?

'Who will rid me of this foul priest?'

The words were uttered and the four knights present looked at each other. Were they being commanded to dispose of the Archbishop of Canterbury? Three of them were uncertain. The fourth?

William de Tracey was an unlikely knight. He came from Woolacombe in Devon, and saw himself as the infiltrator. He felt he had to prove himself in order to maintain his knighthood. His family line was complicated and he was unsure whether his right to his lands was secure – could one of his cousins call him out? The best chance of survival was to please the king. The king would not let down a friend.

Until now. Afterwards, the king would say that the assassination of his good friend Thomas was not his intention. The words uttered were an aside. But to William de Tracey they were both a pathway to the king's favour and the resolution of one of his own insecurities. He had a personal aggravation with Thomas Becket. Many years ago, before either of them was married, Thomas had wooed William's future wife and seduced her. William had no suspicions when he wed his wife that such an association had occurred, and was pleased well enough when a child was born so soon after the wedding. But a casual remark by one of the servants caused him to question his wife's honour. Faced with his rage she confessed all, but could not say who the father was.

Protocol demanded silence. His honour was at stake. Instead, he watched as Thomas became more powerful at court. Each time Thomas looked his way, or even spoke to him, William could feel the shortness of breath, the tenseness in his hands and arms, the thumping of his heart in his ears as he waited for the moment that Thomas would reveal that he had been cuckolded even before he was wed and his heir was not his own. Determined to claim sovereignty over his wife, they had several children in quick succession until it was clear that she could have no more.

The bile and venom rose in his throat each time Thomas walked by, or was mentioned in reports of the court proceedings or even in conversation. And now the king had cried out, 'Who will rid me of this foul priest?'

William thought quickly. The other three knights were all men he knew well, men of Devon who respected him.

William stepped forward. 'Sire, rest easy. Thy will *will* be done.'

The king sat back in his chair and called for a servant to clear the mess, refilled his goblet with wine and toyed with the bread and meat left on his plate while staring into the crackling fire. 'Leave me,' he said.

Outside, William turned to the other knights. 'The king has spoken and it is our duty to comply. We should leave now.'

There was a moment of uncertainty, then, 'The king has spoken.'

The four of them took to their horses and galloped through the night, reaching the French coast. William secured a ship to carry them across the water back to England, to Dover. If the other three knights were surprised at William's determination to carry out the king's will in such a hurry, nothing was said. Maybe, one or more mused, the king, in the cold light of day, would retract the order? But none would admit to it. Maybe some of them held their own grievances with Thomas Becket and also saw this as a way of removing him from blocking their own advancement. We shall never know.

But we do know that while Thomas Becket, Archbishop of Canterbury, was praying in the side chapel of Canterbury Cathedral, the four knights approached him. Thomas had no indication that there was any threat or danger to him. This was the holiest place in all of England and no arms were drawn there. As they approached, he recognised them as part of the king's court. He finished his prayer then stood up to greet them. Opening his hands in supplication, he gave a holy greeting and blessing. Three of the knights hesitated. They were in the house of God. But William stood forward.

'The king's will be done!' he cried out. 'We arrest you in the name of our king and sovereign lord.'

Thomas shook his head. 'The king cannot have sent you. I am too important for men of such low birth as you to come to arrest me. Stand aside and repent your sins.' He stepped forward and held out his arm to bat them away before moving between them.

William was furious. Thomas had spoken the words he had feared hearing all his adult life. That he was not worthy of respect. As Thomas passed him, William grabbed for his arm and span him round. In one movement he drew his sword and ran it through Thomas, who clutched at his side, falling to his knees.

Thomas raised his bloodied hand and cried, 'For God's sake, not here.' But William brought his sword down for a second blow. 'It is not for God's sake but for King Henry who commands this. The Church has no role in the king's rule.'

William turned to the other knights. 'He commanded us all!'

As if they were one, the three knights drew their swords and pierced the body of Thomas. The sun shone through the windows and reflected off the red blood so that it stood out from the shadows.

The deed was done. Certain of the king's favour, they sent word to France to tell of their accomplishment and the freedom the king now had, unencumbered by the Church. They expected to be feted and honoured. They left the cathedral unscathed, and no one tried to stop them. People were too stunned at what had happened.

When the king heard the news he went cold and his hands shook. There must be a mistake. He recalled he had been with the four knights when he received the missive that had angered him so, but he had given no such order. He swore by the Holy Bible that he had no ill intent. But the night's drink did not wipe the memory of uttering these words: 'Who will rid me of this foul priest.' He had said them, and later wondered where the knights had gone, but they were not essential to the running of his court, so he had not given them a second thought. If he had realised they took his words as a command, he would have sent word to stop them.

For Henry, this was a disaster.

When the king's displeasure was made known, William and his fellow knights went from celebrating as the king's vanguard to becoming fugitives themselves. They fled back to their Devon countryside, hoping that family and friends would be able to offer help, support and opportunities to hide.

Convinced of the righteousness of his actions, William went to the Bishop of Exeter for absolution. The bishop had his own reasons for wanting Thomas dead and had some sympathy for William. He advised William to avoid his own lands until the king's position was clear. William went to his cousins at Bovey Tracey and pleaded for their help; they hid him in a cave by Bottor Rock, outside of Newton Abbot.

He was unsure whether he could continue to trust his cousin and the servants, so he moved further north to Crewkherne Cove, near Ilfracombe. He knew of a cave in the cliff's edge, where he had played as a boy. He sent a trusted messenger to his daughter to bring him food and wine, and to call out as if to the seagulls to let him know she was there. It was several days before she came, and William was fraught with hunger. He replied to her call and then, making sure she was unseen, she lowered the basket of goods to him. He quickly removed them and sent back the empty basket.

During this time William reflected. On the one hand, he was satisfied that his honour had been restored and that Thomas no longer posed a threat to him. But now he realised that the king's ambivalence about the validity and strength of his order also put him in a dangerous situation. He could lose everything. He paced up and down the limited cave space, uncertain what to do. His stomach was tight, he had little to eat and he choked on the food brought to him. He damned Thomas Becket for causing him despair whether he was alive or dead.

In the cliff cave he paced the ten steps to the inner far wall and back out to the opening. He watched the seagulls soaring up into the sky. Such freedom. And then they hovered, rejoicing in the updrafts. But nothing to rejoice for William. The long hours of cold and darkness led him to fear the coming morning. He stood on the edge and thought of letting himself plunge down into the sea, to let fate and the fish decide whether he would live or die. He was uncertain whether he was going to heaven or hell for his deeds, and that alone kept him from dispatching himself.

Word finally came that the king had recognised his part and that the knights were not to blame. The king had uttered the words and it was his responsibility as sovereign to ensure that his loyal subjects, who had carried out his wishes, were exonerated.

William emerged from his cave and returned to his family. But never again was he able to look his wife in her eye, and when he heard the cry of a seagull he looked startled as if he had come awake from some nightmare.

Canterbury Cathedral was re-hallowed by the Bishop of Exeter. Some people say that at certain times of day you can see the blood on the stones where the sun shines through a clear window.

Even though the action was demanded by a king, the time and place of the murder was decided by William and the other three knights. The murder in the holiest of sanctuaries was deemed a most foul sin and William was required to pay a penance. After his time in the cave in isolation where he had doubted his own sanity, he was relieved to be able to make things right with his God. Some of the churches in Devon were in a poor state of repair and William was required to provide the funds for this. By 1173, Thomas Becket had many miracles ascribed to him and he was already canonised as a saint. Thus the refurbished churches included a second dedication, to the newly canonised St Thomas Becket.

The irony was not lost on William. In the same year William was appointed to the stewardship of Brittany, so at least the king had forgiven him. But William wanted to make peace with his God and declared that he would make a pilgrimage to the Holy

Land, then return to serve the king and his people. He travelled far but never reached his goal, dying from fever at Cosenza in Sicily. He had said he wanted to be buried in England, but his body was never returned.

Some say that William de Tracey was turned back from both heaven and hell and he is lost in an underworld repenting the sins of his life. Folks do say that you can hear the cries of a lost man down by the Crewkherne caves, or sometimes riding a horse up and down the sands, looking for somewhere to hide.

Lapford Church was one of the churches restored through his graces and it was given a second dedication to St Thomas. Sometimes, after Christmas and before New Year, there can be heard the clatter of horses' hooves on the streets of Lapford. Some say it's William, looking for a place of sanctuary; others say it's Thomas Becket looking for William to get his revenge. But no one will admit to going on the street to find out.

5

The Wrecker's Legacy: Ilfracombe

Just outside Ilfracombe lies Chambercombe Manor. Some say it's the most haunted house in England; others just shake their heads and turn away. On dark nights when there is no moon, there can be seen a shape looking out of an upstairs window. Is it a man, or a woman? It's not clear and yet a faint moaning can be heard.

Life on a coastal shore is challenging. There are those who work on the land and those who work on the sea. There are those who work in the in-between places, which no one else wants to see, where the red-coated excise men try to rout out the lawbreakers and customs avoiders. The dark economy, where the only threat to life is when you are inadvertently spotted by the wrong side and your silence is bought by the gift of a barrel of brandy or the barrel of a shotgun.

But there is an even darker economy than that. The wreckers. On a dark night with no moon, the ships are struggling to find a safe passage along an uncertain shore, laden with passengers and cargo, with promises of riches for those who complete the voyage. Who knows what their fortune is to be?

The wreckers are discreet. Making sure that there are no customs men about, they light their bonfires as an offer of clear passage, a pretence that it is a fairway to a safe harbour. The tired, fatigued wheelman gratefully turns to the shore, relieved that he will have some rest once they have moored up, looking forward to his bunk, crowded though it maybe. Perhaps a little rum in his belly to turn back the cold. But his stomach constricts as he feels the ship shudder and his arms tighten their hold on the wheel. Frantically he tries to turn about, go back into the darkness of the sea away from the leeward shore. Too late, the rock pools and the rising stack towers surface and mislead him. He loses his grasp on the ship, which shakes from side to side, water rushing in, off-setting the fine balance. He calls the alarm to abandon ship and passengers push and pull to ensure they get to the small boats.

The tradesmen on board try to strap themselves to their cargo, while the women grasp boxes and pouches that hold their jewels and try to secrete them on their bodies. It happens too quickly and as the water rushes over the top deck, the mast breaks, tumbling to

the deck, crashing through the wheelman's stand. He tries to hold the wheel, to steer a safe passage, but to no avail. In his last seconds of life he offers up a prayer for his wife, damns those wreckers but mostly shames himself for allowing himself to be seduced by the light that he so wanted to offer his body some respite.

Thus did Alexander Oatway earn a living as a wrecker sufficient to maintain his lifestyle as owner of Chambercombe Manor. They deliberately set lights so that a lost ship might turn to shore and fall upon the rocks. It generated just enough treasure and goods to keep him and his men comfortable, and not so much that his activities could be anticipated and an ambush set. He was a canny man. After all, someone should have the wealth. If a weary wheelman made the wrong decision, better that they should do it on this part of the shore, rather than make a mistake for real and all goods and chattels sink to the bottom of the sea where no man profits. The loss of life was always to be regretted, whether they sank into the sea, or faced his pistol. They all become worm food in the end; such was the cycle of life.

Alexander was very careful and only selected men who were loyal to him. Their successful shipwrecks and generous share from the work ensured their secrecy and cooperation. However, Alexander had been just too canny with his son, William. Hoping to acquire sufficient wealth to pass to his son, William had been given the best education and taught the strictest moral base. Alexander was not going to let his son follow him into the wrecking trade. William was going to be legitimate and Alexander would have the joy of seeing his only son blossom into the ranks of society. His family name would continue for generations and his legacy would grow.

William was now seventeen, an age when he was looking at the family business and starting to dream of the wealth and business that would eventually come his way. But he was puzzled. The accounts did not reflect the apparent wealth they lived in. He resolved to find an answer.

One dark and stormy night, when Bob Bagwell came to the door with a message for his father, William grew curious. He 'retired to bed', then quietly let himself out of the house, waiting under the oak tree, where he had full view of comings and goings. He saw a shadow come out of the front door. As it turned, he could see it was his father. Astonished that the older man would be out at this hour, he followed him. The pathway was tricky and with no moon he could not clearly see the way, but somehow he kept close to his father without being observed.

Something was happening on the foreshore. At first William thought the men were rescuing the poor people caught up in the shipwreck, and he felt pride that his father had come to join them. Then slowly he realised what was happening. The men were plundering the sea to take treasure from the bodies and anything of value that came near the shore. William thought perhaps his father had been alerted to the looters and, brave but foolish man that he was, that he was going to confront them. His mind was jumping around, working all kinds of scenarios to make sense of what he could see.

But no, the men called out to his father. Greeted him with slaps and laughter. His father grunted a few words and the men sprang into action. William could feel the cold tightening of muscles in his stomach and chest as he realised that his father was leading this mob. He gagged and had to hold his hand to his mouth to prevent himself from vomiting. This was against everything that his father had represented. Every sinew was poised to denounce his father but the words were strangled in his throat as he watched as gold and silver were stripped from the bodies washed up on shore.

But then William heard a low moaning. In front of the sheltering rock he saw a young girl, his own age or maybe younger. Her hair and the seaweed were indistinguishable and she struggled to get a firmer grasp on the shore. He saw his father turn at the sound, pull his pistol from his pocket and began striding across the sand and pebbles towards the girl.

A shout from one of the men in the surf distracted him. Three more bodies were washed on the shore and a wooden chest strapped to a pole looked tantalising. Alexander turned away for more interesting booty.

William lost no time. Careful not to be seen, he moved closer to the body. Was it the waves that gave her movement, back and forth, or was she alive and fighting for her life? As he bent over her, a hand gripped the edge of his coat. With no further thought for his safety he grabbed her under the arms and dragged her further on to the beach. Ripping off his coat, he wrapped it around her, lifted his precious bundle and carried it to the house. He called loudly at the door, until his mother and their servant came.

'A ship wrecked on shore,' he gasped. 'I managed to save her from the watery depths.'

He said nothing of his father, as the young girl was taken from him, up to a bed and tended by his mother. It was three in the morning when his father came home to find his house energised by the rescue. His wife greeted him with the news that their son had excelled himself by rescuing a young lady from the wreck. She assumed that Alexander himself had gone down to help. Was there anyone else who needed attention?

William sat in his father's chair by the roaring fire. When his wife had left the room, Alexander spat a twisted whisper to his son.

'I saw you there, hiding in the rocks. What the hell do you think you were doing?'

'Yes, father, I saw you too. I saw you directing the men. And it wasn't about a rescue. It was about leeching everything you could get from the wreck and leaving those souls to the sea.'

'They were already dead; there was nothing to be done for them.'

'Then, father, why did you draw a pistol when you thought one might be alive?'

'Watch yourself, my son. All that stands here will be yours one day and if you want to keep it, then the wrecking brings the jam and the brandy to the table.'

'The wrecking?'

It hadn't occurred to William that his father had enticed the ships in deliberately. He had thought that his father was opportunistically scavenging. Now the gagging in his throat caught him unawares and the wine that had soothed his nerves reappeared to fall to the floor.

William wiped his mouth. 'By everything that is holy, by everything that you have taught me, by everything I believe in! This wrecking is an abomination.'

'An abomination that you have lived well by and don't you forget that. Now, this girl you have brought here. How fares she? Is she alive? What has she seen?'

'Is this all you care about? To save your skin? Well I can tell you this, father, she knows nothing, remembers nothing. She has spoken only Spanish and not coherently. Your secret is safe with her. But I will have nothing to do with you and the riches you purloin from the sea. I will wait until the girl recovers and is at a safe distance from you, then I will leave this house and never return while you are alive.'

Father and son faced each other.

The older man had a grudging admiration that his son had stood up to him, but was bitter that his plans to protect him had now led to this argument. The younger man was torn between loyalty to the father he loved and his utter disgust for the activities his father embraced in his name.

William stayed until the Spanish girl had recovered and arrangements were made for her to return home. Soon afterwards he left to go to Tavistock, where he found work to suit his skills.

Broken-hearted at the dispute between her husband and their only child, the estrangement was heavy on his mother's shoulders. She succumbed to illness and died. Without her support Alexander was a broken man and never led a wrecking again. He sold the manor house and moved to Plymouth where, in time, he died. Father and son were never reconciled.

In Tavistock, William worked hard. If he heard of a family who lost loved ones or chattels in a wrecking, then he was first to attend to their needs. He felt that he had to make recompense for his father's actions in any way that he could. His only friends were his work acquaintances but they became concerned at his reluctance to laugh, or even drink with them. He was persuaded to attend a dance but he spent most of the evening on the edge of the company. His friends despaired of him. But then William spotted a dark-eyed woman, who seemed to be watching him. In a moment of fantasy William thought it was the Spanish girl, returned to seek him out. He approached her and introduced himself, but her laughter and quick wit was pure West Country, although she did confess that her grandmother was Spanish!

Much to the relief of his friends, William took a fancy to the young lady, Ellen, and she reciprocated in her favours. They were quickly wed and in time opportunities for business led him back to Ilfracombe. Chambercombe Manor, now long sold by his father, was available for rent. Moved by memories of his happy childhood, they decided to take on the lease. Somehow he managed to excise the memory of his father on that fateful night. They would build new memories.

Together they had one child: Kate, with dark eyes and hair like her mother and the same determination, grit and high moral ground as her father. William took her on long walks in the country where he reminisced of his childhood and of his desire to own the manor should ever his fortune allow.

William's business prospered, and one day a young Irishman named Wallace hobbled into his office. He had spent time at sea but, after an accident on the ships, he now walked with a limp. He hoped that his leg would recover and he could return to the sea, but in the meantime he sought work on shore. It suited William to employ the man both for his experience at sea and for his pleasant manner with the customers.

In the meantime, Kate had grown into a young woman and her dark looks attracted attention. Having been brought up in a strong Christian household, where adherence to the law and society was held above any personal interest, she was very interested to hear of the stories that Wallace told of his experiences on the ships. Pirate ships. Was that the life he hoped to return to?

William was shocked to learn of his senior office clerk's life in the dark economy and he sacked Wallace. But to William's horror, Kate had formed an attachment with him.

It was Ellen who found the note.

My loving parents.

You have given me so much and now I will seem to disappoint you.

I love Wallace so much and I will marry him. He says that thanks to your guidance he has given up his pirating days and wishes to return to Dublin to find his fortune in a legitimate way using the skills you have taught him. And I want to be with him. I want to be by his side. I want to be like you, father, helping the wayward to stay on the path of righteousness. Bless me and I will return to you in time and with good fortune.

She was gone. William beat his own breast at having exposed his daughter to the temptation, and his wife consoled him. He hoped and prayed that Kate's husband would have the will to avoid the path of damnation, unlike his own father.

There was no word from Kate. It was as if she had slipped away from their lives. Now two lonely people walked together in the fields, reliving the times they had been with their daughter. The way she had run up to them with daisies in her hands and they had made daisy chains. Or the time she had found a small bird, fallen from its nest, too injured to save, but she had held it in her hands until it breathed its last. William shared the stories he had told Kate of his dreams of owning the house of his child-hood. Somehow he hoped that if he could buy the house, she would return home to them. There was no logic in that, but it seemed so important to him.

Five years passed.

Storms came and went. Ships passed down the channel. Sometimes the wreckers drew in a ship; sometimes it was nature's own doing. William and Ellen did the best they could to help anyone caught up in the wrecks. Some bodies they laid out for burial. Some they pulled alive from the sea. Some they nursed in their own home. William felt he had much to atone for his father.

One night there came news of a ship out to sea that was strug-gling to make safe harbour. William and Ellen were down on the shore. There was a woman whose body was washed up, her arms stretched in front of her. They each grabbed one arm and pulled her to the shore. Her face was badly broken; her jawline had been penetrated by a broken mast. But she was alive.

William bent down, encompassed her in his arms and took her back to the house. They placed her in one of the upstairs bedrooms. Ellen stripped the woman of her wet clothes, notic-ing the broken ribs and the copious blood coming from her wounds. As William took the wet clothes from his wife, he felt something drop. Lifting the skirt up, he found a small oilcloth bag. He looked up at his wife. She was tending to the woman in the bed, washing the blood around the raw open wound on her face. He opened the bag.

It was full of gold coins. In a flurry he searched the rest of the dress and sure enough he found another three, stitched to the underskirt. He could hardly breathe as he opened each one. There must surely be two hundred gold coins. No wonder the woman had been weighed down in the sea and so easily crushed by the flotsam and jetsam.

The woman gave a moan. Ellen turned up the oil lamp and the woman on the bed reached up and grasped her hand.

'Money.'

The word was hardly distinguishable, so distorted was her face, her mouth torn away.

'Oowse.'

That was nonsense. What was she trying to say? Her hand gripped Ellen's. And then let go.

Two hundred gold coins. That would be enough to buy this house. William had a germ of an idea. What if she died? Then there would be no one to claim the money. He could have everything that he wanted. With a start he realised that he was now thinking like his father must have done, all those years ago. He shook his head, to throw the thought away. But it stayed there. Niggled at him. He whispered to his wife.

'Will she live? Will she die?'

His wife threw him a look, as if he was cursing the woman. He spoke again.

'She must be in great pain. Should we let her go now? She would have such injuries that she could not live long. Would it be kinder to end it for her now?'

His wife shook her head.

'She is someone's daughter, someone's wife, someone's mother. You would wish them to lose her as we lost our daughter? We must help her live. If she dies it is God's will, not ours.'

In his mind William was racing ahead. If they could buy this house, then maybe he could get a message to his daughter and she could return. He'd even put up with her husband if he was a pirate.

He looked down. The basin was full of bloodied water.

'Get some clean water,' he said. His wife took the bowl and stepped out of the room.

The woman in the bed was clearly distressed, finding it hard to breathe. He held her hand, but she could not grip any longer and he could only feel how the fingers had lost all their muscle tone.

'I'm sorry, my dear,' he said. 'I know you are in pain and you will lose your life soon enough. I will use your money to good effect. It will reunite my family. In your death, new hope for me is born. Go now and be released.'

He took the pillow from under her head and pressed it down on her face. There was no struggle.

When Ellen returned to the room, the woman had died. The pillow was back in its usual place. His wife wept.

'We will have to give the body up tomorrow,' she said. 'The shiremen will come calling to see if we have given shelter to anyone.'

'If we do that,' said William, 'we will have to give up the gold. No, we will have to bury her ourselves.'

On the next morning the shireman was knocking.

'William. A bad night last night with the shipwreck. Were you out at all? Did you see or find anyone?'

'No,' responded William, 'none at all.'

'Well, there was a ship that floundered, but most of the passengers are accounted for. Only one woman was washed overboard. Apparently she was a local woman, returning home. Wanted to look out for her father and mother. Well, if you see or find anyone, let me know.'

The shireman turned away, but Ellen came to the door.

'The lady. Does she have a name?'

The Shireman checked his papers.

'Katherine Wallace. She was a widow.'

Ellen fainted.

The woman upstairs was their daughter. And William had ended her agony. If only he had known. They would have cared for her, let her recover, maybe even to speak to them.

But for two hundred pieces of gold he had thrown that all away.

And now they had a body to dispose of.

Years later, there were reports of footsteps running up and down stairs, a gasping and then a wailing. But no one was ever seen and it was never clear where it was coming from.

In 1865, Chambercombe Manor was being renovated when workmen discovered another room at the top of the house which had been boarded up. When it was opened, there was a bedchamber, with a four-poster bed. On it was the skeleton of a woman and beside her were four oilskin bags. No one knew who she was and eventually she was buried in the churchyard. Did William and Ellen board up the room where their daughter lay?

To this day, the footsteps and moaning can still be heard.

6

A DEAD MAN'S REQUEST: SPREYTON

It was the summer of 1682. The country was settled after a long period of strife. At the age of twenty, Francis Frey was a manservant, happy enough in his work for his new master, Mr Phillip Furze, and yet feeling the need for a challenge himself.

His master's father had recently died. Francis had never known his own father. He'd been born in the workhouse and then taken as a skivvy when young. He took guidance from whosoever offered it and then disrespected it as he chose. He remembered the old master fondly. Cracking out orders, expecting Francis and the other young servants to 'jump to and get the job done'. The old man had an obsession with his gardens and lawns. Freed from the austerity of the Puritans, he had lavished his money and created a thing of beauty. But the annual invasion of moles would send him into a furious rage and he would take his very long and robust stick and try to wheedle them out of the ground. It was Francis who got left with the disposal of the bodies. 'My right-hand man,' said the old man, 'I know I can count on you.'

And so it was that, as he rode into North Tawton, Francis caught a glimpse of a man at the side of the road, too well dressed to be a beggar. As he drew closer the hands that held the reins of his horse so confidently started shaking.

It was the way the man stood, with the long stick that Francis remembered so well. The hat. Francis swallowed but his mouth was too dry. It could not be!

'Hold up, young Francis,' called the man at the wayside. The voice. Francis knew that voice.

He pulled up his horse and looked down. He knew those deep penetrating eyes. He'd seen the curve of that nose silhouetted against the sky since he was a young lad. He knew that lank mane of hair, even on occasion being called to comb it through.

'Master?' he queried. 'Master? What are you doing here?'

His breath was shallow in his chest, as the words tumbled out. He knew this man. He and five others had carried this man's coffin to the church next door.

'Young Francis, my lad, I am the same. Your master of old but returned for this day to make sure that son of mine plays true to my wishes. It is cold there in the earth, and none more so when you can see the world passing you by as if you never existed. But I made my promises and my son must deliver. So tell him he must make good and pay to Squire Arnold the ten shillings I owed him, and the ten shillings to Archibald Common.'

Francis could see the flaw in this.

'But sir, Archibald Common died the day after you. No money can be paid to him.'

'Take me for a fool, do you? Archibald had a wife and children. Tell my son he pays them the money. And also my sister in Totnes. I made no provision for her and it weighs heavy on my heart, so tell him to pay her twenty shillings so I may rest easy in my grave. For if you do not do these things, I will come back for you. Do you understand?'

Francis nodded. 'But sir! Who am I to tell my new master what to do?'

The old man before him laughed. 'Say these four words and he will know who sends you.' There was a whisper and an exchange of nods. 'You are a good boy, Francis. My right-hand man. I can count on you. Do not let me down.'

With that the old man started to turn, and then had a second thought. 'Mark you well, if you do not do these things, then my second wife, the bloodthirsty hag, will have her way with you and there is nothing I can do to hold her back. I do not know what it was in life that you did to her, but in death she wants her revenge. I can only hope that by helping me, you can assuage your fault with her. For your own good, do as I ask.'

And then the old man was gone.

Francis turned his horse and rode back to the manor house at Spreyton. He told his new master everything that had happened. The master gripped Francis's collar and pulled it back, asking if Francis was trying to obtain false monies from him, but as soon as Francis said the four words, he let go. His eyes flared wide, his mouth aghast. He shook. Then he apologised, reached for a bag of coins and asked Francis to fulfil his father's tasks.

The monies were paid to Squire Arnold (who was mighty pleased to get the money), and the widow of Archibald Common, who was overwhelmed to get an unexpected windfall.

There was one final task. The sister in Totnes. His master wrote a letter and Francis handed it over in her sitting room. She read it, gasped and dropped the letter in the fire beside her.

'When did he make this bequest?' she drawled. 'For I was at the reading of the will and I heard nothing for myself. Is this out of pity that my nephew sends me the offering?'

Francis saw no other way but to tell her how it had all come about.

'A dead man's promise! Never!' she said. 'I want no part of it. It's devil's money. Return it to my nephew.'

Francis was flummoxed. He had tried to fulfil the promise but to no avail. It was too late to make the return journey that night, so he was allowed to remain in the servants' quarters.

And it was there that Francis found himself being poked in the ribs by something like a wooden stick. He woke thinking this was a trick by the other servants, but they were snoring either side of him. None of them appeared to be awake.

'Ow!'

Francis was on the receiving end of a blow again. He looked up from his pallet and closed his eyes, trying to deny what he had seen. A third jolt and he was fully awake and on his feet.

There was the old man. Again. A bit more shimmery this time. Almost transparent.

'Please', whispered Francis, in case he woke the other servants. He didn't want to get a reputation as a man who travelled with ghosts. 'Please be quiet! What do you want?'

'My sister! You didn't give my sister the money.'

'I tried but she wouldn't accept it. I did my best!'

'Ha, lad. You don't know my sister. Use the money to buy a ring. She'll take it then. Then I promise I won't bother you any more. But I warn you, fault me on this and I cannot protect you any more from my second wife.'

Francis wasn't taking any chances. The next morning he requested to see the gentlewoman and suggested the compromise. To his surprise she was quite taken with the idea of a ring from her brother's money, and as it would be chosen by the young man in front of her, she would be so disposed to accept it. She described the ring she had in mind.

The ring was purchased and duly delivered. With his heart feeling a lot lighter that his task had been completed, Francis got back on his horse and made for home, away from the fleshpots of Totnes. At least he had escaped pursuit by the ghost of his former master's second wife.

But never, ever take things for granted. As Francis's horse came back into Spreyton, a shudder of cold went through him. His horse faltered for a moment, then neighed frantically. Around his waist Francis could feel a creeping chill and a pressure under his ribcage. He looked down to see two long white hands, either side of him, making their way to entwine their fingers. Something was behind him on his horse.

His breath came in short bursts as he struggled away from them but their grasp seemed to be even tighter. His lungs strained to draw in fresh air. At the point that he feared he might black out, he felt himself raised up from the horse, suspended in the air. A crackling sound and then a thunderous noise. Francis found himself on his back, in the dirt. On his horse there was a white-haired harridan. Long fingers and long nails, at the end of very long thin arms. Her hair was a mass of rampant spiders' webs and her jaw jutted away from the rest of her face. Was this the ghost of his deceased master's wife? He had not known her in life but now it seemed that despite everything, she had come to haunt him. Or at least something had.

And haunt him she did. Francis was frantic to understand why this demon should take against him. He had complied with everything that had been requested of him but strange things started to happen. For a while there were just random creaks in the house and maybe a jar or book would be moved when no one was there. Even a barrel of salt went from one room to the next and no one would say how it could do that.

Then, one day, Francis felt a pain in his head, as though someone had caught him in a vice. Unable to concentrate he felt himself dragged head-first across the floor, coming to and finding he was rammed between the bedhead and the wall. His muscles cried out in pain as he tried to free himself. He was fixed so tight that he thought he might possibly die there. His faint cries for help were finally heard and it took two men all their strength to free him.

There was neither rhyme nor reason to the attacks. No one wanted to be anywhere near Francis. They didn't want to be the next victim. Francis was at his wits' end. There was nowhere to go. Nowhere to run to. No family and the only friends he had were those who cowered away from him, afraid lest they too should share his plight.

His head was bleeding from being trapped, and one of the maidservants bandaged it. But even as she finished, the bandages were seen to unwind themselves and then encircle him around his waist. The memory of the tightening while on his horse came back to him and he screamed in fear as the bandages slithered around his waist once, twice, three times. Pulling. Tightening. The fear was etched on the maidservant's face. She made frantic attempts to pull them away, only to have them encircle her own wrists and hold them fast.

The house was built adjacent to the church grounds, and a doorway on the side meant it was easy to slip out to reach the church for sanctuary. One night the visitations were so bad that, at daybreak, Francis crawled down the stairs. As the birds greeted dawn, he let himself out of the side door and painfully made his way into the church, where he pleaded with the priest for holy water. Thus sanctified, Francis felt his limbs loosen and the tension seemed to exit from his body.

He stayed in his bedroom with the holy water by his side. Slowly Francis began to recover and he vowed to leave that house as soon as he could, to try and make his fortune elsewhere.

But the vengeful ghost was having none of it. When Francis felt better, he ventured outside the house. He breathed the fresh air in deeply, grateful for the chance to fill his lungs. In front of him he could see some leaves stir off the ground, swirl in a circle, then bring in more dirt and debris. He watched them, delighting in their peacefulness. He sighed in relief at the normality of it. Then he realised they were coming towards him. By the time the swirl reached him, it was so powerful it sucked him up into the sky. He struggled to breathe. He tried to hold on to anything within reach. The windowsill, the door frame. Even the eaves of the roof. But it

was no good and he was raised up. Francis went limp and sobbed, giving himself up to this demon ghost, lamenting and wondering what he had done that he was tormented so. He had no idea where the ghost finally laid him out. All he could think was that he could take no more of this treatment and he wanted to die.

The other servants saw him taken but were so scared that they did not tell anyone until the next day. The priest was adamant that they should search the nearby woods to see if they could find him. Surely a puff of wind or a demon could not carry him so far? Following the last direction he was seen, the villagers scoured the wood for him.

'Francis? Francis Frey?'

It was at sunset that they heard a voice. Singing praises to God, then berating the world around him. They found him in a quagmire, almost up to his neck. Trapped. Held there. Hardly able to breathe. He was unable to recognise his rescuers, so addled was his mind. He thought he was a babe again, wrapped in the swaddling clothes, held in a manger. With great difficulty and great gentleness, they managed to release him. He was taken to Crediton, where he was nursed and cared for. They bled him every day and he continually complained of a tightness around his chest as though a metal band had been placed there. He had fits and delusions, once saying that a bird had crashed through a window and hit him on the forehead with a stone. While the bruise was there, there were no other clues as to what really happened. He never left that place again.

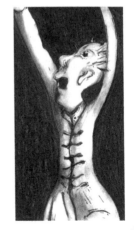

And so it was. Francis Frey was the victim of a malicious ghost. He had helped his master after death, but faced the malice of the dead man's second wife, who inflicted her wrath on an innocent man.

Or maybe there was more to the story than ever we should know?

7

THE LEGEND OF BENJAMIN GEARE: OKEHAMPTON

The night that Benjamin Geare was born there was a thunderstorm. Lightning cracked across the sky, illuminating the darkened fields. The farmhouse had candles alight at each window to welcome in the new child; the midwife had been summoned. In the adjacent stables, the old mare readied herself for the birth of her foal.

Both mothers cried out as their babes thrust through the wombs into this world. Both babes had a cord around their necks that stifled their breathing. The midwife improvised: she had seen this before and knew to cut the cord quickly and breathe life into the child. An old superstition, but it worked and soon the lungs of the small babe were exercising themselves to the full.

Not so in the stable. The old mare was unable to help her foal and even though she neighed for help, the other horses could not help her, locked in their stalls. The stable lads were focusing their attention on the main house, anticipating the feasting and festival that would follow if there was a son for the household. The baying from the old mare was lost, and so too was the foal. Black it was, but unable to take a breath in this world. The old mare, exhausted from her struggle and in despair at the death of her foal, gave up her last too.

But in the house, they were rejoicing. A son was born. The midwife wiped the blood from the babe's head and placed him in his mother's arms. She held him tight and looked up at her husband, who beamed from ear to ear, delighting in his dynasty. There was a party such as there hadn't been for a long time. The three little crosses in the churchyard would not be joined by their brother just yet, and the two elder sons looked forward to teaching tricks to their new brother.

When the old mare and her foal were found dead, the farmer beat the stable boys about the head for neglecting their duties, but his pride got in the way and the meat from the carcases was roasted. The heart of the foal was given to the mother of the child as a delicacy and thanks for the safe delivery. The irony of that was not lost on her, as her new son drank heartily from her breast.

'Drink, my little one,' she said. 'May the soul from the colt drive you onwards.'

Benjamin's two older brothers tried to blame him for all their mischief. But whatever they tried, somehow Benjamin was one step ahead of them and the brothers found the tables turned on them when they were punished for Benjamin's tricks.

Out in the fields Benjamin spent as much time as he could with the horses. Running by their side over the fields, puffing and panting to keep up, and riding them bareback, knowing no horse could buck him off. At the end of the day he whispered to the shy horses to bring them in.

As he grew up, Benjamin became notorious for having his thumb in every pie. If there was some endeavour, a meeting, a party, or even a new enterprise or business, Benjamin was there finding out all he could; sharing the information, bringing people together for mutual benefit, slapping each other on the back and maybe supping a glass or two of wine. He was equally at home in the offices of the town hall as in the coffee houses and social establishments.

Benjamin went into merchant trading. He, like many people, invested his money into ships bringing cargo from the Far East, Africa or the Americas, gambling that when his ship came in the profits would fall nicely in into his pocket – which they did many a time. But pirates were rife on the high seas, and if they took your cargo and your crew you could lose everything unless you paid them a ransom.

In Okehampton, local merchant tradesmen decided to counter this by contributing to a fund to help each other if their ships were held, and they looked for someone who was an honest, upright man to hold it for them. Benjamin was so well regarded that he had been made mayor five times over. On the third time he stood, people talked of it being a one-horse race. With Benjamin in the starting stalls there was no need for anyone to enter. It was agreed that he was the best man to do the job.

He was 'honest and upright' until it came to the day when all three of his ships failed to come back into harbour. He tried to hide the fact that his fortune was gone by falsely using the insurance monies to buy new ships and restock them with new cargo, hoping to spin a healthy profit and pay back the money as well as rebuild his fortune. After all, pirates wouldn't strike twice, would they? Sadly, they did. Benjamin was left without his fortune and had used all the mutual funds for his own benefit.

His name and reputation were at risk and he did not know where to go. Some say he turned to the Black Arts to win back his fortune. Some say he entered into a pact with the Devil. Some say he simply had a broken heart. Whichever way it was, Benjamin was struck down with a fever.

The doctors were called in, but despite all of their potions and lotions Benjamin took a turn for the worse. One evening, with the air crackling with lightning and thunder, his wife wiped the sweat from his brow. He tossed and turned, calling out. He rose up from his bed and, whinnying loudly, he leaped over the foot board and ran around the room, foaming at the mouth, looking like a wild animal trying to escape the confines of the house until he collapsed in a heap. His wife and one of the servants struggled to get him back to the bed but he thrashed about, trying to get away from them, his eyes wide open but unseeing.

His breathing became erratic, fast, as though he was racing and then slowed down. He was sweating profusely. As he died he gave a great cry. One local man was riding his horse home when it stopped in the roadway, shook its head and neighed so loudly the man thought his horse was possessed. The next day there were reports of horses that had gone to one side of the fields in the night, shaken their heads and had neighed spontaneously in unison.

There was a funeral. Benjamin's coffin was placed on a carriage hearse, drawn by four black horses. They set off by themselves with no man needed to lead them, walking in stately fashion through the town to the cemetery. But by the time they reached the graveyard, the coffin was gone and with it Benjamin's body. People were aghast! No one had seen it fall out, or anyone remove it. It was as if the carriage and horses had moved through an invisible curtain and the body was gone. With nothing to bury, the townspeople were perplexed as to what they should do. The vicar held his Bible high and called them all to a memorial service, where they would pray for Benjamin's soul and ask for the return of his earthly remains.

That should have been the end of it. But with no body in a burial site to anchor to, rumours began to circulate around the town that Benjamin had been seen. First the reports came from the coffee houses, where he was seen drinking, and then the town offices where he would walk through, perusing the open files and ledgers. He was even seen walking down the streets, smiling and nodding to people passing by whom he had known in life. It was most disconcerting. Even as he passed the horses on the road they snuffled and snorted, with a shiver over their flanks.

The rumours spread beyond Okehampton. People were either driven away by the stories or, in some cases, attracted by them. Either way, it was not good for business. Representation was made to the vicar. He was completely bewildered. Nothing like this had happened to him before. He sought advice from the archdeacon, who nodded his head. This was the kind of thing he had experienced and he instructed the vicar as to what he should do.

At the time between day and night, when the sun just goes down and the birds quieten, when the curtain between this world and the next is at its thinnest, the vicar used his bell, book and candlestick to summon the soul of Benjamin Geare. As his old friend stood before him as a bewildered spirit, the vicar wanted to offer him words of comfort but knew he must be strong and lay this ghost. He said the words of the exorcising ceremony, praised the Lord and offered solace to the spirit of Benjamin Geare, but nothing happened. No laying of the ghost. This was not working. Benjamin's spirit was becoming restless and started to move away. The vicar called to him again, but to no avail.

The vicar realised that there was something more going on than he could cope with. Benjamin's haunting of the town was too intrusive. Trade was being lost, and people felt that it was an insult to the Church that his ghost would not be laid.

Summoning up all his willpower, the vicar called to Benjamin's ghost. 'Make retribution for all your sins. Cast yourself upon the mercy of God. Repent and do penance.'

But to no avail. Benjamin's ghost turned away; no mere vicar held him in thrall.

Benjamin's haunting of the town became increasingly intrusive. No one was sure when he would arrive. Ladies in the street, with their purchases, would suddenly be accosted by a ghost. Their breath caught in their throats. The muscles in their arms froze and a deadening tightness overcame them. They dropped their parcels and fainted away. Gentlemen would be conversing in the club, or even on the street, and Benjamin would appear among them. No matter how much they tried to hide their feelings, their hands shook, their throats dried and those with a stick rested more heavily. When Benjamin's ghost walked down the aisle of the church, the vicar conceded defeat. First there would be a cold chill in the air. A sudden breeze catching your cheek, when nothing else moved, then a book would move or a candle would blow out. Five more attempts were made to perform the exorcism, five more men of holy orders, but despite much use of incense, holy water and rhetorical bluster, none of them worked.

Visiting the archdeacon was a priest who had seen many spiritual possessions and ghosts laid to rest by prayers in other faiths. The risks were high but he was prepared to help the people of Okehampton, who could not sleep at night for fear of the wandering spirit.

He prepared himself by fasting for three days. His body was taut and ready to stand up to the Devil if he had to wrestle him for the soul of Benjamin Geare. He prayed before the church altar then waited in the market square. Benjamin Geare appeared before him in his ghostly form. The priest began to say the prayers and the litany of saints.

He intoned, 'I cast you out, unclean spirit, along with every satanic power of the enemy, every spectre from hell and all your fell companions; in the name of our Lord Jesus Christ. Be gone and stay far from this creature of God.'

Nothing seemed to be happening. The priest reached out his hand and then, taking inspiration from within, he reverted to a language that the Good Lord would have known. In Arabic he cried: 'Be at rest, Benjamin Geare. Thy journey here is done and we celebrate all that you have done for us. Thanks be for your gifts and sacrifices, we shall share and honour them.'

As those words echoed around the streets, Benjamin's spirit seemed to change. There was something in his ghostly eye that could have been fear or could have been excitement. Whichever path he was taking, the ghost of Benjamin Geare said, 'Now thou art here, I must be gone. I am unconstrained.'

Benjamin's ghost began to move and lose shape. The priest was certain that now the spirit would be released and make its way to the next world. But to his astonishment, it changed into the form of a black horse that reared up, snorted and gave such a neigh that people in the next county could hear. It dropped to the ground and galloped through the town, creating as much mayhem and havoc as if it was alive.

Ghosts of men were one thing, but ghosts of horses were another. Let us say that this priest had some unusual ideas and there were consultations with some practitioners of the Black Arts. A different kind of plan was formulated.

A bridle was found that had never been used and was sprinkled with holy water. The priest sought a young man who was still 'innocent' of the world and instructed him to approach the ghost horse and to offer the bridle. The curiosity of the horse would enable him to capture it, they said. He was to mount the horse and then ride it as fast as he could to Cranmere Pool in the middle of the moor. There the waters had already been sanctified with holy water and prayers.

'Ride the horse into the pond but mind you leave his back before he hits the water. And whatever else you might do, do not look back at the horse.'

With the streets cleared, the young man walked forward and waited. With no one else to distract him, the ghost horse soon found him. Quaking inside, the young man knew his duty and put out his hand. The ghost horse came closer and started to nuzzle his hand, until in a sudden movement the young man had the bridle over the ghost horse's head and slipped on to his back. With the bridle in his hands, he turned the horse's head and rode towards Cranmere Pool. He urged the horse on and on, and the beast went faster and faster, as though the Devil was after him. And maybe the Devil was, because as rider and horse approached the pool, the lad urged the horse into the water then let go of the bridle on the horse's head and tumbled off on to the ground at the edge.

With a soaring leap, the horse landed, front hooves first, into the pond and went down, down, down into the depths of the pond, never to be seen again.

Despite all the warnings, the young man turned his head and watched as the black horse entered the pool. As the last hoof disappeared into the water, so did the young man's sight. He was found the next day, trying to find his way back to town. In appreciation of his sacrifice, the townspeople gave him a home and cared for him for the rest of his life.

Benjamin Geare? As man or horse he never bothered the town again.

There are many variants of the tale of Benjamin Geare. Some have him weaving sand, others have him emptying Cranmere Pool with a sieve until he fills it with a sheepskin and then scoops out the water. But they all agree on one thing: he was a memorable character and he definitely haunted the town!

8

THE SILVER INK POT: HAYNE MANOR, STOWFORD

Henry Harris rested in his brown leather armchair, feeling very contented. Around him the shelves creaked with the books of his lifetime interests. He prided himself as a man of science and investigation and congratulated himself on being invited to join the Royal Society of London. The times were a-changing and with Queen Anne upon the throne, there were many exciting new scientific developments happening. A thought occurred to him and after contemplating for several moments, he determined that he would write to his colleague to ask his advice on the matter. He rose from the chair and moved to his desk. The writing papers were in a folder on the side and he opened the writing box to get out the pen and the ink pot.

He was surprised to see that the silver ink pot was not in the writing box. He searched again, taking all the items out one at a time, then putting them back in. He looked on his desk but it definitely wasn't there. The floor perhaps?

His butler came into the room, with his afternoon cup of coffee.

'Ah. My silver ink pot. Do you know where it is?' asked Henry.

His butler looked at him. 'No sir, it's not anything that I deal with. Perhaps you have mislaid it? I think I did see a glass ink pot on your desk.'

The butler was right, of course. There was a glass inkwell on the desk and Henry wrote his letter thinking no more of it.

That evening, when he was dining with his wife, she mentioned that there had been a silver salt bowl that had gone missing. A glass one was now in its place but she had rather liked the one that her aunt Agatha had given her. Henry remembered the silver ink pot and wondered. A worm of suspicion was wriggling in his head and he was thinking back to a conversation he'd had with her a few days previously.

Both the butler and the footman were in the room serving dinner. By the time they had finished the second course, the little worm was now of a substantial size. Henry indicated to the servants that they were dismissed. As soon as they had left the room, Henry turned to his wife.

'My dear, do you remember a few weeks ago you had said that you had misplaced your silver hairbrushes?' She nodded. He pressed her further. 'Did you ever find them again?'

'No,' she said, 'and now you mention it I have lost other silver pieces. Hairpins, even a bracelet that you gave me for our wedding. I don't wear it but I like looking at it. Altogether not worth too much but I imagine it all mounts up.' She gasped. 'Do you think that we have a thief within the household?'

He shook his head. 'I don't know but it can't be a coincidence that all these things just disappear. We shall have to look into it.'

Over the next few days, Henry and his wife reviewed all their personal belongings. They found that several items made of silver had vanished. Sometimes an alternative was in its place, so that the function was always preserved, the hair was always brushed but the recipient did not always notice whether it was with a silver brush or plain wood.

Mrs Harris then requested the servants to take out all the silver plate dining service and polish it for her review. While they normally had ten to dine, they had place settings for twenty. Now they only had twelve.

'This is very serious,' said Henry. 'We must find who is responsible.'

That very evening Henry and his wife summoned all the servants to their drawing room. The butler, the housekeeper, the cook, two maidservants, but only the second footman.

'Where is Roger, the other footman?' was Henry's opening question.

The cook spoke up first. 'I haven't seen him since yesterday,' she said, 'I asked him to get me some herbs from the kitchen garden and he didn't come back.'

'Anybody else seen him?' asked Mrs Harris. The servants shook their heads.

Henry turned to the second footman. 'You, you share a room with Roger. Any sign of your room-mate?'

The young man blushed and looked at the ground.

'Speak up, the master has spoken to you!' snapped the butler.

'He said only that he had some concerns and wasn't sure who to speak to!' The footman looked back at the ground.

'I wonder what concerns they were?' snarled the butler. He turned and looked at the assembled company. 'If any of you have any concerns, then it is fit and proper that you come to me. My door is always open.' He nodded and looked at them in turn. Each of them looked away.

'Thank you for that,' said Henry. 'We have discovered that a great deal of silver plate has gone missing from the house. Small pieces that normally we wouldn't miss. It's been taken over a long period of time. And we want to know who is responsible for this?'

Suddenly Henry felt very inadequate as a man of science and investigation. This wasn't going quite as well as he had imagined it.

'Well sir, if I might intercede,' said the butler. He tilted his head and a small smile danced across his lips. 'I think the fact that the footman is missing might be a clue to your culprit. He was in the dining room the evening you asked your wife about the silver brushes. And when you tasked us to polish the silver, he may have been tipped off. I don't think you need to look any further.'

Henry was flummoxed. Regrettably, he had to come to the same conclusion. The footman was probably responsible for the thefts and he had flown. Without the man there, there was no chance to confront him and get a confession. They were unlikely to retrieve the goods. Time to draw a line under the matter and be more diligent in the selection of their servants.

A week later Henry awoke alone in his bedroom, his bed-clothes strewn about him. His pillows were on the floor. He put his hand up to his eyes and rubbed them.

After breakfast he took his wife aside.

'My dear, it's most extraordinary. I had a dream about the young footman.' She gave him a quizzical look. 'The one who stole our silver plate. I dreamed he was standing at the bottom of my bed.'

She laughed at him. 'Dearest, it is only a dream because you are so distressed at being deceived. I myself wake at night and remember something else that he has stolen. I could not sleep but for worrying. I now have paper by the side of my bed and jot things down. As soon as the words are on the paper, I am gone to sleep again. I am sure it will pass.'

Reassured, Henry placed pen, ink and paper by his bedside. 'I will write this vision away.'

Sure enough, as soon as he fell into a deep sleep, he opened his eyes. And there, standing in front of him, was the footman, this time halfway between the foot board and himself. Henry tried to think of what might be worrying him, so that he could write it down, but the footman just stood there, staring at him.

Henry reached out to the young man but his hand grasped air. The footman remained standing, looking into Henry's eyes. His face held no emotion. Henry felt he was expected to respond in some way. He tried to sit up but then he awoke again, entangled in his sheets.

Henry was unsure what to do. As a man of science and investigation, ghosts and spectres were not to be tolerated. And indeed the young man must surely be alive, having left the manor house only a week previously with his haul of silver plate.

His wife had shown him no sympathy, so he rode over to see his friend the local doctor. There he explained his dilemma. The doctor, of course, took a different point of view and offered him a sleeping draught so that he could rest through the night.

Henry took the draught and retired to his bed, expecting a good night's sleep. But it seemed to him that no sooner had his head hit the pillow, than he was awake. The ghostly apparition of the footman was standing by the side of his pillow.

Henry struggled to find words. His throat was tight and he found it hard to breathe. 'What do you want? Are you real? Or are you a figment of my dreams?'

The footman stood there, stared again into Henry's eyes, took a step back and waited. Then he took another step back and waited again.

'What is it?' rasped Henry. 'Do you want me to follow you?'

The figure gave a slight bow and gestured as if to invite Henry to his side. Henry slid from the bed, pulled on his boots and wrapped a coat around his shoulders. 'All right,' he said. 'Take me where you must!'

The floor creaked as he walked across the room. The footman seemed to give off a light so that Henry could see his way. At the door the ghost stood waiting, until Henry reached out his hand, grasped the door handle and pulled it open. In an instant the spirit was on the other side. Henry stepped out into the hallway and followed him until they reached the stair banister. Henry breathed deeply.

You'll be all right. He doesn't want to hurt you.

At the top of the stairs he hesitated.

If he wants to harm me, this would be the place to trip me, let me fall and then break my neck. Is it revenge the footman seeks?

To his surprise his companion, step by step, lit the way for Henry until he was on the ground floor. Henry felt more confident that he was safe but where was the footman taking him? To the main door, unlocking it and then standing on the hearthstone, with a full moon illuminating all about him.

Nothing stirred. No calls of the fox, no cries of the owl, no snuffling of the badger. Even the trees held their branches still as Henry was led across the estate to the far side.

I know this part of the estate. Nobody comes here anymore. Somewhere near here was an old oak tree that was dying and my brother and I would squash inside it. It was our hiding place.

The footman stopped in front of an old oak tree. Henry caught his breath.

This was the tree, the very tree. Am I just dreaming, remembering childhood games?

The footman gestured inside.

What does he want me to see? It's too dark.

The footman waited.

There was nothing else to do. Henry would have to return in the morning. To make sure he could find the tree again, he slipped off his jacket and then tore a strip from his shirt to tie around the branches. He turned to the footman.

'That's the best I can do until morning.'

The next thing Henry knew was he was on his own bed, with muddy boots and wearing a torn shirt. The sun was peeking through the curtains and the butler was regarding him anxiously from the foot of the bed.

'Come on!' shouted Henry. 'We must find my shirt!'

Saying nothing to anyone, Henry sent word to his friend the doctor to help him investigate this strange experience. The doctor arrived with the vicar and soon the three men were striding across the grounds, accompanied by the butler and the second footman.

'Here is the tree,' said Henry, as he caught sight of the remnants of his shirt, fluttering. It was much as he remembered as a child and he set his feet on the bark to test out the entrance to the hollow trunk.

He called to the butler. 'Come on, man, you're younger than me. Start from this side and when you get to that branch, twist over and you can see down into the middle of the tree.'

The butler blanched and shook his head. 'I cannot do that,' he said. His hands were shaking and he looked as though his knees would give way beneath him.

'Oh, come on man,' said Henry, crossing his arms and breathing in through his teeth. 'It's no different from when you climb the ladders to get into the attics or storerooms. Just climb up there and look. Tell us what you see!'

The butler continued to make his excuses, until the second footman stood forward and offered to do it. Up the tree the young man went and then twisted over the branch to see inside. He reached in and felt around. He gasped and then jerked his arm away. His hand had fastened on to something that was now caught on his sleeve. He screamed and tried to shake it off. The object came back over his head, crashing down to the ground in front of the butler.

'Merciful God!' cried the priest.

'Damnation!' cursed the doctor.

'Roger!' cussed Henry.

The head of the missing footman was before them. Caught up in his hair was the missing silver ink pot.

The butler was on his knees, sobbing and asking mercy from God for all his sins.

It took a while to get the body out of the tree, along with all the silver plate that had gone missing. The butler confessed that he had been stealing the silver plate for some time but it was not until the silver ink pot had gone missing that the losses had been detected. He had stashed it all in the hollow tree, confident that no one would go there, but Roger had followed him and demanded half of the hoard. They had fought and the butler had used his knife on Roger's throat to silence him.

The butler was hanged for his crime. Henry had quite a story to tell at the Royal Society.

Some people say that on a moonlit night, Roger the footman can be seen in Hayne Manor, walking along the corridors, or even in the grounds. Some people say that he carries his head. All I can say is that Henry knew that there was more on earth than just science and that sometimes you have to put your trust in the unknown.

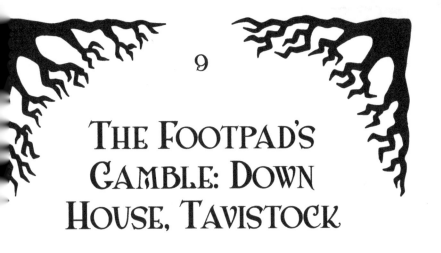

9

THE FOOTPAD'S GAMBLE: DOWN HOUSE, TAVISTOCK

I don't know quite how it happened. Solomon and I were outside of town at Tavistock, waiting to catch some fancy gentleman out walking and relieve him of his goods. Footpads, some call us; others aren't so shy and call it street robbing. As far as I'm concerned, it's easy money in my pocket! Puts food in my gut and pays for the bed we share. I like to take my bludger with me – a good club that's nice and quiet to use – and it don't cost as much as a pistol. They are too easy to drop and lose if the punter puts up a fight. Give me a bludger any day. Solomon prefers the long knife – his hanger – but sometimes he can be a bit fancy with his handiwork and I don't like that. I've not killed anyone yet and I'd plan to let it stay that way!

We'd thought it was easy pickings when we saw the fat gent and his lady as they strolled out. Solomon was taken with the idea of threatening the old gent with his hanger. Sometimes he likes to draw blood on their cheeks as he persuades them to hand over their purse, watches and maybe a jewel or two and leaves me to threaten the lady. That generally gets the goods handed over. Except this lady was a doxy dressed to the nines. As soon as I realised what she was, I knew her bully boys must be close by, so I shouted to Solomon that we had to go!

Too late! As soon as there was a cut on the gent's cheek, the doxy's men were there. I knew how it would pan out. They would claim they were rescuing him from us footpads and claim a reward. Money in their pockets and no risk to them. And there were four of them.

We set to but it was obvious we were outnumbered. One minute I was giving them what for with my bludger, when I felt a sudden pain, a knife slicing through my guts. I lost my breath and then my balance. I heard Solomon cry out behind me. A gurgling noise, like water trying to gush free. I dropped to my knees; I could feel the cobbles underneath as though they were huge rocks digging into me. I slid to the ground, cracked my head and there were stars shooting across my eyes. I felt a loud drumming in my ears, then a sound like the wind whistling. The muscles in my body felt like they were unravelling, becoming frayed and then seeping out of me into the ground below and to the sky above. All I could see was blackness and in the distance a flickering light …

The next moment I was sitting on the floor in front of a roaring fire in a tavern. Opposite me was a table with these two men sitting with their goblets of wine and bread on a plate in front of them. One was a really old man, bald with a pure white beard, although you could just see flecks of dark hair. He seemed to be dressed in some kind of robe that was sometimes silver and sometimes kind of rose-gold. My eyes went bleary just watching it change. He had an axe by his side. I couldn't quite see if there was blood on it. I felt queasy and I didn't know what to make of it. The other man was younger, dressed in red and black silks and satins. I swear he had a gold tooth that shone in the reflection of the fire. He had a pitchfork at his feet.

At first the two didn't take any notice of me, but took their time to drink their wine and take it in turns to break the bread.

'It's an interesting one,' said the older man. 'Technically he is right on the border between you and me. He's never actually killed anyone. A point either way and it would be clear but that's not happening.'

The other man laughed. 'Well look at his record. He definitely belongs to me. Don't give yourself so much grief. Just hand him over and you'll never have a second thought about it.'

Sitting in front of the roaring fire felt warm and comfortable. Not too much of my life has been like that. My mother had come to the workhouse for shelter. They told me she was thrown out of her job at Down House because I was in her belly. She begged them to tear me from her womb when she couldn't bear the pain but she died anyway. No one knew who my father was, although I was told later that some people thought it might have been one of the men at Down House. But to a child growing up under the care of the workhouse, these are just things you hear about, as you try to manage from day to day. You dream of someone coming for you. But when you live in there, you don't even know about mothers and fathers. You take what comfort you can from the person next to you. And even a beating feels like a promise of love.

To be honest, I scarpered from there as soon as I could and went to live on the streets, scavenging food where I could. I don't like to talk about the things that happened to me, or the things that I did to others. Let's just leave it that I gave as good as I got so I reckoned I was even.

For some reason the couple in the brandy shop took pity on me and allowed me to sleep out the back at night, while during the day I collected the pots, swept the floors and cleared the pissing places. Yes, I probably got into some dodgy deals but I was always fair to the landlord and his wife. I know about not messing on my own doorstep. If I knifed anyone, it was only because it was in self-defence. But no one is interested in hearing that from someone who was brought up in the gutter. I always kept myself clean of trouble when I was working in the brandy shop.

'Ah, William. You are awake!' said the old man, turning towards me.

'We were just talking about you!' laughed the other man. 'My friend here wants to take you to his place but I think you'd rather fit in with me. Several of your friends are there – John, Bernard, Titus and even Solomon. You'll want to join them, won't you? They are dancing in hell as we speak. Then you can drink and fight as much as you want! You'd much prefer that, wouldn't you?'

He laughed again. 'You would, wouldn't you?'

I thought of John and Titus from the workhouse. I hadn't seen them in a long time and my hand ached from the scar that Titus had left me as a reminder of what friends were about. Bernard and Solomon were good mates, nearest I had to anyone I could call brother and they always had my back. Solomon was with me in the fight, so I couldn't work out how he'd already gone with this man. But Bernard had been hanged three months gone. I was confused. But I'd follow those two anywhere.

The old man put his hand up. 'Don't say anything just yet. My dear friend, Lucifer, will try any trick to get you to agree.'

The other man laughed. 'Jude, you never give up, do you!'

Jude smiled in return. 'That's why I'm the saint for lost causes, Lucifer, and why you are the devil to pay!'

The old man turned to me and said, 'This is an unusual situation. You have died and we sit at the last tavern before you reach the fork in the road to the pearly gates or to the fiery doors of hell. The checks and balances of your life are on a pinhead. You could tip into hell, or make it to the gates of heaven. And we are here to discuss the relative possibilities.'

Lucifer lifted his finger. 'To cut him short: the choice is yours. Be reunited with your mates! Come with me to hell and you will have a roaring time. You won't know anyone in heaven – I've checked the inventory. Even your father is down in hell – you'll meet him there!' Lucifer grinned. He had more than one gold tooth. It looked as though a flame flickered from one to another.

Jude shook his head. 'First things first. Lucifer is right. In this moment you can choose to walk away with him. Many who have sat at this table have done that without a second thought. But on that pinhead is a cacophony of angels, who want you to have a second chance. And so this is the deal.

'You can go now, down to hell. But if you want a chance for heaven, you can go back, for a year and a day. You can haunt one specific place and in that year you cannot speak until you are spoken to.

'If you are spoken to and if those words invoke the Devil, then straight to hell with you. If the words invoke the name of God, then you may choose to come to heaven. You always have the choice. Of course, if they say nothing, then it's straight to hell.'

Jude turned to Lucifer. 'Do you want to add anything?'

Lucifer smiled, his lips curling back over those glistering teeth. 'And no haunting before sunset, or after sunrise!'

Jude frowned. 'That's not in our contract!'

'It is now!' Lucifer turned to me. 'William, come and meet your friends! Or go to heaven, be by yourself and watch those do-gooders turn away from you because of the things you have done.'

They both looked at me. Waiting for my response.

It was obvious. Go where you're wanted. That's what I thought to myself. But then the mention of my father made me stop. I remembered the couple who ran the brandy shop. They were the closest I'd ever had to family. All right, he cuffed me hard when I did something wrong, but there were times he sat with me over a drink and we'd talk or sing together. He'd offer me advice about the ladies, then give me a stern look over his tankard and say I wasn't to bring any back to the house for his wife's sake. I didn't like to tell him it wasn't the ladies I was interested in. His wife sang to their children, pulled their hair in jest and held them tight, while I watched and listened. When they fell over and grazed their knees, she wiped the blood and kissed their tears away. It was times like that I wondered about my mother. If she had lived, would she have done those things for me? What would it be like to meet my mother?

I turned to Jude. 'Where is my mother?'

Jude asked. 'Where do you want her to be?'

'I never knew her but I hope that she is in heaven and not hell,' I replied.

'Then I am sure that is where she is. Unlike my friend here, I can't tell you that. I will just point out that Lucifer didn't mention her.'

I made my decision. 'I'd like to try for heaven.'

Lucifer slammed down his goblet on the table, wiped his mouth and muttered under his breath.

Jude smiled again. 'And where would you like to haunt? One specific place.'

I thought about it. Where might I go? The workhouse? The brandy shop? Where was the one place I always wanted to go but never did? Then I knew.

'Down House,' I said. 'I've never been there. Maybe I can find out something.'

Down House. The place where I had been rammed into my mother's belly. The household that had spurned her when she was in need and denied me a father. It wasn't what I expected. A desolate place on the edge of Tavistock, halfway from the town to the moors. A house just big enough with fields and pasture for a farmer to make a living. Neither was there anyone living there who could have given me answers. It was harvest time and during the day there were the travelling men who came to help with the crops, but in the house were a young farmer and his wife and their two young children. I'd forgotten that Lucifer had already said my father was already in hell.

It was a mistake. I should have gone to hell to find him there.

I wasn't really sure what I was supposed to do. I thought I would just have to turn up, do some ghostly things, they would say something and it would all be decided. But I spent a long time working out what I could do – walking through walls, floating up the stairs. I found I had to be anchored to something physical, I couldn't just hover in the air. It was tricky being a ghost.

The first time I appeared in front of them the sun had just gone down. I'd watched her put the children to bed. Tucking them in. Kissing them on their heads. I liked the way that she did that, I never had anyone do that for me. I decided there and then I wouldn't haunt them in the house, I didn't want to scare the children, I'd stick to the yard. Get the job done. The mother and her husband sat on a bench in the yard, watching the sunset. He smoked a pipe. I didn't want to startle them too much, so I just emerged from the shadow. I knew they could see me. She just stood up, put her hand out to her husband, he took it and they went into the house. I couldn't believe it. Not a word said to me.

Of course, I could still go inside the house, so I went in after them, kept in the corners where they couldn't see me.

'Did you see the lad in the yard?' asked the mother.

'I saw the ghost of one, if that's what you mean?' the farmer replied.

'He looked so sad and confused,' she said.

'He's never been here before – why now?' wondered the farmer.

'Perhaps he's lost his way?' she said, wistfully.

'Take no notice of him, let him alone. If he comes out when we are in the yard, we'll come in. We won't speak with him, we won't interfere with him. He wafted in here, he can waft out again. Are we agreed?'

'Agreed,' she said.

Of all the places to choose to haunt, I had to pick one where they didn't talk to ghosts. Sometimes I didn't care and thought I'd be going down to hell anyway, so I bided my time. There were nights when I thought I wanted to get it over, so every time they went in the yard after sunset, I would be there and I tried to frighten them just to say something. But they were as good as their word and turned away from me and went back into their house. They did all their tasks before sunset, so there was nothing left to do outside.

Of course, during the day I could see them, they couldn't see me. The farmer had plenty of work to do, so when he left the house, he was gone for most of the day. But the mother worked so hard with the chickens and the pigs, clearing the yard, then doing things in the house as well as keeping an eye on the children. One was a little boy and his name was William too. The other was a girl called Nancy and slightly bigger. I would pretend I was the boy and I would get closer when the mother was with him. When the farmer came home he would lift each of the children in turn, up into the air and swing them around, then tumble onto the beds and play peekaboo. I felt so relaxed when they all were together. Are ghosts allowed to smile?

During the night I wouldn't go into their home. Once they'd gone to bed, I'd explore the yard, the pump, the pigsties and sheds. Trying to imagine the work my mother would have done.

I found that I could let myself go down into the ground and found there were underground springs, a cellar and something very surprising underneath the pump.

The year was passing and it was harvest time again. Soon my year and a day would be up. I no longer wanted to go to hell. There was someone else I wanted to meet. But I didn't know how to get the mother and the farmer to speak to me.

Lucifer came to see me, with his flashy red and black satins and silks, with his golden teeth glittering in the sunset. 'Tonight,' he said, 'is your last chance. If they don't speak to you, then down to hell with me. The boys are waiting for you!' He laughed.

For the first time I could smell something – and it wasn't pleasant. I remember once Solomon and I stole a suckling pig and tried to roast it ourselves. But we burned it, the flesh was charcoal as we ate it and it made me retch. Lucifer carried this same smell about him. I thought of John, Titus, Bernard, Solomon, even the man who was my father, and for the first time prayed that I would not be joining them.

There was a cry from the house. Young William. I turned away from Lucifer and was in the boy's bedroom, in the corner again, out of sight. His mother was there with her hand on his brow. His father in the doorway.

'Mother,' the boy rasped, 'I feel so hot. May I have some more water?'

She looked into the jug by his side. It was empty. Turning to the farmer, she indicated the jug. He shook his head.

She frowned and said, 'I'll get you some, William. I promise.'

Taking the jug herself she went down the stairs. Her husband tried to dissuade her.

'No ghost is going to stop me getting water for my son,' she said.

She wrapped a cloak about her and stepped into the yard. The farmer stood in the doorway, watching her. I saw my last chance and took it. The pump in the yard reflected the full moon. It was almost as bright as day. She strode over to the pump with the jug in her hand. I appeared between her and the pump. She stepped to one side, as if to avoid me, but I moved again. She stepped to the other side but I kept myself between her and the pump.

'In the name of God,' she cried, 'why do you trouble me so?'

In her desperation she had broken her vow and spoken to me, calling on God's name. I was overwhelmed to hear her words. I wanted to embrace her, thank her. But now time was short.

'It is well that you have spoken to me in the name of God,' I said, 'this being the last time allotted to me to trouble this world.'

I didn't know what else to say and I stepped aside. She placed the jug under the pump and forced the handle up and down. The water gushed out.

I knew I would leave soon and I desperately wanted to say farewell to both of them. They had become so important to me. I had witnessed a mother and father's love for their children. It had changed me. I wanted to give them something back. She filled the jug then, without taking any notice of me, she turned and strode back to the door, where the farmer was still standing. Then I remembered.

'Now do as I tell you,' I called out, 'and do not be afraid. Come with me and I will direct you to something that will remove this pump. Under it is concealed a treasure.'

She took no notice of me; she went straight inside the house and up to William's bedside. The farmer stood by the door, hesitated, then stepped out, following me. I indicated to him to find a crowbar, and then lever away the water pump. As I watched he strained to do that, but as he finally toppled it over he gasped as he saw a cache of gold coins hidden underneath. Just as I had seen.

'Spirit,' he said in awe, 'what do you want me to do with this?'

I had a fancy that the gold had been stashed by my father, for my return. Nonsense, of course – I was far from anyone's thoughts when the money was buried – but it suited me to think it was mine to give away.

'Use it,' I said, 'and stock your farm. Take care of your children and let William and Nancy grow strong and prosper.'

He took off his shirt and started to fill it with coins.

I wanted to give him something more. I was on a roll and I decided to make a promise. Jude could sort the details out later.

'Listen,' I said. 'If any person molests you or otherwise threatens you on your property, only call on God.'

'Thank you,' he said, 'and God bless you.'

'No,' I replied. 'Thank you for changing my death.'

The cock crowed.

I felt my spiritual form fade, almost drop to the ground; and then, like a murmuration of starlings, I rose up towards a cloud that was struck rose-gold by the rising sun.

10

Lovers by the Gravestone: Killworthy House, Tavistock

Eulalia Glanville sat at the breakfast table, hands shaking, tears running down her cheeks. Her uncle had sent the servants from the room. She looked at her aunt for reassurance but the older woman craned her neck to look out of the window.

'He is a good man for you to marry,' declared her uncle. 'Joshua Heath is a wealthy man who has a good business as a goldsmith. He sits on the bench with me. It will be useful to have our families allied and I know that I will not have any financial concerns for you. I will settle a dowry on you so that you have some independence, more than your father left you.'

He paused and glanced at his wife but she deliberately carried on watching the birds in the sky. He continued. 'I've been talking to him for some months now and he would be willing to marry you in April.'

Eulalia turned to her aunt and reached out her hand. Mrs Glanville gave her a glance then looked down at her plate, the knife and the fork placed at a precise angle to the side. Crumbs and a smear of jam were the only evidence of breakfast. She would not let herself catch the eye of her husband's niece.

With no ally in the room, Eulalia chose her words carefully. 'Thank you uncle, for your consideration. However, I have met Mr Heath only once and I do not know if I can live with him as a wife should.'

Mr Glanville scowled. 'Do not try to talk to me of love. This is a business proposition that secures your future. I care for you but I have several children of my own to provide for. You will enter into this marriage and give him at least two boys for his heirs.'

'Two boys? Am I to be a breeding cow for him to have heirs?' gasped Eulalia.

'Don't use that language with me,' retorted Mr Glanville. 'You are not your mother! She was a Spanish whore who persuaded my brother that you were his child but when he died he left you nothing. I took you into my house when you were ten years old. I have cared for you as one of my daughters and this is how you repay me. I have other responsibilities and I can no longer support my brother's …' he paused, then finished, 'child!'

Eulalia reared up, her chair falling to the floor behind her.

'Sir,' she said, 'I'm sorry that I have been such a drain on you and your family. It was never my intention to be such.'

'I want none of your mother's temper here. I have long accepted you as my brother's daughter. If I do not care for you, then no one will.'

Eulalia fled from the room. Outside, her cousin Elizabeth was waiting. 'What did father want?'

Eulalia felt the tears flow. 'He tells me I am to marry Mr Heath. He's an old, old man who is thin and scrawny, with a dreadful beard and ghastly breath. And I don't love him.'

Elizabeth put her arms around her cousin. 'It's father. It's his way of being fair. This way you'll be settled for life.'

Eulalia pushed her away. 'You knew!' she gasped, 'I thought you were my friend, my sister. But you knew and you did not tell me.'

Eulalia stood at the bottom of the stairs in Killworthy House and wailed at the betrayal from the family she thought of as her own.

At midday, Eulalia dressed warmly and walked down the hill into Tavistock. The road was winding and steep but she knew every step of this path. And every step took her closer to Michael.

She had been in the church cemetery, laying flowers on her mother's grave, when she had tripped and fallen. Her ankle was painful and she could not get up again. That's how she met Michael. He was a lieutenant in the Royal Navy, home from the sea, also visiting his mother's grave. Seeing her distress he had come to her side. With no one else around to assist he had asked permission to remove her shoe to see the damage and, always practical, Eulalia had agreed.

As his hand had touched her stockinged ankle, she had felt a wave of pleasure flow up her. She had flushed and turned away, with her breath coming in short spurts.

'Your ankle seems well, nothing is broken,' he had said. 'Give it a moment and then you'll be able to stand.'

He had escorted her back up the hill, offering his arm for support and then taking her up to the house. The servants had come running when they saw her and swept her inside.

Distraught at not being able to thank the young man, Eulalia had tried to struggle back to the door, but he had gone. She wondered if she would see him again and took the first opportunity, when her ankle was healed, of going back to her own mother's grave. There was nothing there, but then she recalled the direction he had come from and went to look for his mother's headstone. She found a bottle partially buried there. Inside was a note addressed to her. She scribbled a reply and thus it was that messages went back and forth, and they eventually met again. Now she wondered if her uncle had heard of their illicit meetings and had decided to marry her off to get her out of the way? Or was he just a man with four daughters whose welfare and marriage prospects he had to put first?

Whichever way it was, Eulalia was determined that she would not be the wife of anyone but Michael, who, it seemed to her, was the only one who paid her any attention and consideration. When she told Michael what her uncle proposed, she was surprised when he didn't share her anger. Instead he was quiet and did not speak for several moments.

'This man, how old is he?' he asked. Eulalia was surprised at his question. She said she believed him to be about sixty.

'Then if you married him and he died, you would be entitled to all his wealth?' She replied that she imagined that would happen.

'Then would it be so bad if you married him, took him to his bed to strain his heart through "energetic exertion", so that he died and left everything to you?'

Eulalia was shocked. She had not considered the prospect of marriage to Heath and had thought that Michael would be so enraged, that he would sweep her away and they would live together forever. Energetic exertion? What did he mean? And why should she marry the old man? Michael explained to her that he had only his living as a lieutenant and no money to provide for her when he was at sea. If they married they would be as poor as church mice and at least the mice had a roof over their heads. If she was a rich widow, things might be very different indeed.

Mr Glanville was delighted when his niece agreed to the wedding and Mr Heath came to the house to meet his bride. As they sat drinking tea together, chaperoned by her aunt, she was aware of his odour that mingled the scent of tobacco with the essence of whisky. It revolted her and she turned away from him when he tried to kiss her to seal their engagement.

The marriage was planned soon enough. Michael was due to return to the sea for a voyage that would take him away for several months. She was able to get away for an afternoon, and Michael introduced Eulalia to what she must expect as a wife. With him she found it most pleasurable. She was greatly fearful, however, of the prospect of meeting her obligations with her new husband as well as taking part in sufficient 'energetic exertions' to strain his heart. Michael assured her that it was simple to manage. He taught her how to tease, withhold favour and then when the old man was exasperated, to make an offer which the old man would seize with extreme enthusiasm, thereby putting pressure on his heart.

Michael went away. The marriage happened. Eulalia perfected the skills that Michael had taught her and found, to her horror, that the old man seemed to thrive on such a relationship.

When Michael came back from sea, he found Eulalia in despair. The old man showed no signs of dying and seemed healthier than ever. She was more afraid that she would now produce the heirs that her uncle had insisted on. 'Will you still love me,' she whispered to Michael, 'if I carry another man's child?'

Michael realised that discretion was needed. He told Eulalia that he knew a woman, Maria, who could act as her maid and carry messages between the two of them. They could no longer meet as they had done, otherwise their plan would be unmasked.

Maria soon entered the Heath household as Mrs Heath's personal maid. At long last Eulalia had someone to confide in. She had felt so lonely since the day she had quarrelled with Elizabeth Glanville. Maria took letters back and forth nearly every day but Eulalia very rarely saw Michael.

Over the months, Heath remained healthy and robust, until finally Eulalia declared she could take it no more. She wrote to Michael. 'My bloods have stopped twice, and I feared I was with child. Maria has a certain way with herbs which have restored me. I cannot bear letting that foul beast use my body. We must do away with him and then we can be united.'

Michael suggested they use monkshood to be rid of the old man, as Maria knew how to find and crop it. At first Eulalia was shocked and demanded a meeting with Michael. They met at the graveyard, with Eulalia attended by Maria. It had been several weeks since she had seen him and the two lovers embraced while the maid kept watch for onlookers. Michael reassured her that the plan was good and this would be an efficient way of getting rid of Heath without causing suspicion. Maria would administer the herb to the whisky that Heath drank each evening. Eulalia agreed, thinking only that she would soon be with her lover. As she and her maid left, she did not see the brush of hands and the gentle twist of the fingers between Michael and Maria.

Suffice to say, everything was done: Heath died and Eulalia came into his estate. After the funeral and the reading of the will, she visited her uncle's family, sharing the news of her good fortune and her plan to move to the Americas, taking only her maid and a manservant. Elizabeth was pleased for her cousin but sad that she was departing, while Mr Glanville could only reflect on the turn of events that his niece was now a financially independent woman. He was relieved that all had worked out for her.

That was when the nightmare started. One day Eulalia chose to go out in her carriage by herself to purchase a gift for Michael. She arrived back at her house, slipped in through the front door and up to her room. She opened the door to find Maria, in a state of disarray, trying on some of her dresses with Michael sat encouraging her. Eulalia's fiery Spanish temperament finally got the better of her. She screamed at Maria and tried to tear the

clothes off her. 'You are dismissed. Leave my house. Leave my man. Leave everything.'

Michael wrestled her to ground and held her there until she stopped screaming, then kissed her until she calmed down and embraced him. His excuses were flimsy but she loved him so much that she didn't try to make sense of it.

But the damage was done.

Maria was now out on the streets and fearful that she might be accused of the death of Mr Heath. She went to the authorities and revealed the entire plan with the monkshood and the whisky. If she was not to get her man and a share of the money, then no one would. The depth of the plan was revealed, with Maria having been Michael's lover since before Eulalia had met him. Eulalia had been deceived all along.

Eulalia, Michael and Maria were charged and put on trial. By one of those twists of fate it was her uncle, newly appointed to the judges' courts, who was asked to oversee the trial. He had a reputation for being fair and meticulous and he felt he could best serve his niece by demonstrating his rigour of interrogating the evidence, so he agreed. Alas, the evidence was overwhelming and stood up in court, even when the judge suggested supplementary lines of questioning to the defence.

The three of them were found guilty and given the death sentence.

It is said that Mr Glanville, although he continued to serve as a judge, wandered the grounds of the old Killworthy House, broken-hearted that his diligence led to the death of his niece.

And his niece can be heard howling with rage at the bottom of the old staircase.

The old Killworthy House was burned down and rebuilt in 1852. The new build is currently a school. Most variations of this tale say that Judge Glanville prosecuted his daughter but the records show it was his niece who was found guilty of the charge. The unsigned typed manuscript at the tombstone of Mr Glanville, in the Tavistock parish church, gives more detail and suggests that the actual timeline for some of these events is a little out, but nonetheless this is essentially the tale that is told and oft repeated!

11

TWO SISTERS:
BERRY POMEROY

Eleanor was thrilled. She was five years old and her mother, Lady Pomeroy, had promised her a baby brother to play with. She was so excited.

'When will he be here?' she asked. Her mother had smiled and patted her stomach. 'Soon.'

When her father came into the room, Eleanor ran up to him. He smiled and reached down for his daughter, lifted her up, then swung her around! Her dark long hair flowed behind, catching him in the face.

'A son,' he cried. 'I'm going to have a son. And you will have a brother to play with.'

Her father took her to the window and looked down on the castle courtyard. There was a woman searching through the ground straw, looking for eggs, pushing the clucking hens out of the way. A man scrubbed down a horse, paused to blow up its nose then laughed as the horse shuddered and raised its head to neigh. Two girls and a smaller boy ran through the legs of the men trying to build a wooden lean-to. The children scooted into the kitchen door but were swiftly booted out by the cook, but with a crust of bread in their hands.

On the other side were the ramparts with the guardroom. It was her favourite place. The guardsmen all stood up when she went in. She liked that. It made her feel as important as her mother and father. Sometimes they lifted her up to look out of the slit windows, to see more soldiers drilling there. They sang songs and she danced to their tune, or just stood in the corner, breathed in the smell of their sweat and the odour from their leather jerkins. But sometimes they closed the door on her and said, 'Not today.' Those were the days when her father looked stern and was quite cross with her, so that she hid behind her mother's skirts.

She loved it best when she sat while her mother sewed. A wooden frame held the cloth and her mother showed her the embroidery. Sometimes Eleanor tried it herself but the needles were awkward and she couldn't handle them properly. Her mother laughed at her struggling and said that when she was older she would be able to do it. She would then stroke her hair and Eleanor would arch her head back and stretch her spine as though she was a cat, blissful in the attention she was getting.

She knew about cats. The cook kept one in the kitchen. One day her mother had taken her to see it in a basket in the pantry. Eleanor put her hand out to stroke it, as she had done many times, but the cat spat at her and dashed out her claws, making a weal on her hand. Tears had welled up and Eleanor had turned to her mother for comfort. But her mother had pushed her away.

'Watch!' she said. 'See how big the cat is. She is going to have some babies.'

The cat started moving in the basket, contorting itself into a more comfortable position and then the muscles all over her body spasmed in waves.

'Watch!' her mother repeated.

From under the tail came a small furry thing covered in sticky stuff. Eleanor was fascinated. She'd never seen anything like this come out of a cat's bottom. The cat moved over, picked the scrap up in her mouth, moved it closer to her, then started licking it clean. A tiny little kitten. Then another and another.

Six in all. The cook stood close by, wiping her hands on a cloth. A bucket of water stood by her side.

Eleanor stretched out to pick up one of the kittens, but her mother restrained her.

'No,' she said. 'Not yet. They are so new. Their mother will want to keep them close.'

'Not so close, my lady,' said the cook. 'I have no use for six kittens, especially the girls. We'll keep the boys and then dispose of the rest.' Her foot hit the bucket to indicate her meaning.

The words meant nothing to Eleanor. All she could focus on was the tiny little creatures.

'May I keep one?' asked Eleanor.

Her mother smiled. 'No, you can't have one of these, but you can have something even better. You are going to have a brother to play with and look after.'

Eleanor had woken in the night. She had a dream where she couldn't find her mother and searched through the castle for her. She had woken up and called for her. No one came but now she could hear screams echoing around the castle.

She tumbled out of bed and drew her clothes around her. Out into the corridor. The torches were still burning and there were women running up and down the stairs. The screaming came again. This time she recognised it.

'Mother!'

It was a long and difficult birth. Unnoticed by the concerned adults, Eleanor had slipped in the door and stood in the corner of the room. This was nothing like the tranquillity of the cat giving birth. She put her hands over her ears and watched as the baby was torn from her mother, placed on her chest and then winced as the infant searched for and found her breast.

'It's another girl.' The women muttered to each other. 'His lordship won't like that.'

Eleanor waited to see if any more babies came. None did. She'd been promised a brother but there was only a girl. And she knew what happened to mewling girls.

The baby was named Margaret. Her mother no longer sat at the embroidery table but on a chair, holding the baby and stroking the blond hair.

'You are so pretty,' her mother cooed.

When Eleanor tried to push her way into her mother's arms, she heard the whisper, 'Not now dear.' Eleanor longed for the time when her mother stroked her hair in the same way.

Her father was not happy. He raged at his wife over his need for a son. Eleanor watched as several times her mother's belly swelled and then lost its shape. But no brother came.

Yet all the time her mother told her youngest, 'I want to keep you close.'

Her father had no time for his eldest daughter. He no longer swung her around as he had. His concern was only to ensure the future for the family and their lands.

As Margaret grew bigger, she began to follow Eleanor around the castle. Everywhere they went, the servants would stop and admire young Margaret. Eleanor tried to push her away but Margaret would only keep closer. One day Eleanor could hear music and song from the guards' room and she ran to join them. As she got to the room, she could glimpse Margaret dancing inside and then the door was shut in her face.

When Eleanor was ten years old, her mother died from yet another failed pregnancy. Now she had to put away childish things, while Margaret played on.

It was after her seventeenth birthday that her father summoned her to his room.

'I have been impressed with the way you have run this place efficiently and well after your mother's death. As you know, I must make provision for our family fortune, and with no son it will fall to you as my eldest daughter to hold these lands and marry well so that our family line might continue. My friend, Lord Arthur, has a son, Hugh, who should be a suitable match. With this in mind I have arranged for young Hugh to visit here. Be courteous to him. Court him as much as he courts you. And then all these lands will be yours.'

Eleanor was delighted. She knew the young man and had seen him at some of the social gatherings. He was not particularly good looking but he had a certain air about him that encouraged a young lady to get to know him better. This pleased her a great deal. It also crossed her mind that at long last she would now be in a position where Margaret was no longer her equal but merely the sister of 'her ladyship'.

The invitations were sent to Lord Arthur and his son, and Eleanor had the pleasure of preparing the house to welcome her potential husband. She was in her element and in the odd moment she had to spare, she reflected how her life would change when married; and, more to the point, she allowed herself to wonder about marriage.

'Will you kiss him?'

Eleanor was shaken from her thoughts by Margaret's question.

'Pardon?'

'Will you kiss him?' Margaret asked again.

Annoyed at the intrusion and embarrassed at her sister's accuracy of knowing where her thoughts were, Eleanor thought to dismiss her.

'What do you know of kissing?' she asked.

Margaret laughed. 'More than you know, dear sister. And Hugh is a very good kisser, I'm sure!'

There was a vein in Eleanor's neck that throbbed, as she drew in her breath. She raised her hand to hide it. There was no point in letting her sister know how agitated she was feeling. She decided to ask her father when the marriage would take place. Eleanor wanted it to happen as soon as possible.

The servants told her he was resting in his room. She climbed the stairs, and when she stood outside the door she paused, then knocked on the door.

'Father?'

There was no reply. She pushed open the door, in case he might be sleeping. And screamed.

He was lying face down on the floor, with one arm outstretched. She called for help but it was too late. He was dead.

After the funeral, there had to be a period of restraint while the household mourned. Hugh had come to the castle each day to offer his support, but Eleanor thought he was more likely measuring up the strength and worth of the lands and castle, anticipating what he might own on marriage and have at his disposal. But she did not mind. The contracts drafted by her father meant that she was to be well provided for even if her husband had control of the land. She sighed. She loved this place.

Her sorrow was for the loss of her father and her mother. She would walk from room to room and along the ramparts to the guardroom. So many happy memories and then a sharp cut as she felt those memories subsumed by her sister's smile, especially when she was taking something from her. First their mother, then their father, even the banter of the guardroom. But now she would be mistress and her sister would be at her beck and call. Perhaps now would be a time to build bridges with her sister. Start afresh. Each knowing where they stood.

She made her way towards her sister's room but stopped outside when she heard laughter inside. Male laughter. A sound she knew too well.

The door was ajar and she looked inside. Her sister stood by the window and kneeling in front of her was Hugh. In his hand there was a ring, a love token. Her sister bent down towards him, took it and kissed him on the lips.

'Are you sure that we can marry?' asked Margaret.

'I have confirmed it with the lawyers. Your father's contract only says his daughter. It does not specify Eleanor, although it is implied. But it is legal to interpret it either way. We can marry and you will be mistress of this castle as well as my heart.'

There was more laughter and sounds that Eleanor could not bear to hear.

The fury rose up inside. Her sister was stealing what she most wanted. She did not understand why her loins ached but she knew that Hugh's seed would never lie there. A future of joy and happiness that had lain before her was snatched away by her sister. Again.

The following day, when Hugh arrived, she summoned him to her drawing room. She told him that until the house had finished their period of mourning, she felt it unseemly that he should continue to visit. Despite his protests of love and desire to support her, she declined and made it known to the housekeeper and guard of arms that he was not to be admitted until all the formal mourning had ceased.

That evening she went to her sister's room. She thought that if she professed her love for Hugh and how she was looking forward to marrying him, that maybe Margaret might stand aside. As she spoke, she could see Margaret's smile curving over her face and she knew there was no point. Eleanor returned to her writing desk, took the quill and ink and wrote a note. She summoned her maid.

'I have received some correspondence and here is a letter for my sister. Please take it to her but don't let her know it comes via me.'

The maid bobbed and took the letter to Margaret. She opened it and read the words. 'We must elope,' the letter said. 'I cannot live without you for one more day. Let us go away, wed, then return to claim our lands. Hugh.'

She could hardly believe that Hugh was planning to come to the castle that very night to take her away. It did not for one minute occur to her that it came from anyone else than Hugh. He had said all the things that were in her heart and she longed for him.

The note told her to meet him at the top of the dungeon stairs. The dungeons had long been abandoned, and no one went there. He said that he had learned of an old gate and pathway into the castle and they could leave undetected by it. She half-remembered her sister having told her stories about such a path when they were children and she wondered at his diligence in exploring the old story.

With joy and anticipation she packed a bag and at sunset, as requested, she made her way to the top of the dungeon steps.

She thought of the time when she had caught Hugh's eye. Smiling and preening at him, drawing him away from her sister, encouraging him to be bold and bolder in flirting with her. Shivering with anticipation, she waited.

Someone kicked a stone and she turned towards it. It was not Hugh but someone else in the shadows.

'Who is there?' she called.

Silence. Then footsteps on the stone floor, pebbles underfoot scattering away. Hands around her head, tight, so tight, and then battering her head against the stone wall.

A voice rasped, 'You will not have him. Not him. Not anything. None of this.' Each word a beat, each beat a thump against the stone wall.

Margaret tried to raise her hands to protect herself, push her assailant away. But the pain in her head was so great, her eyes fluttered and she lost focus. She clawed the air for balance, caught something and heard a tearing of cloth. With one almighty thrust she managed to gain space, as her attacker stepped backwards. She tried to push past, and run back up the stairs. She cried for help but was seized again and a cloth stuffed in her mouth.

'He is mine, do you hear. Mine. This place is all mine.'

Dully, she knew this was Eleanor. And an Eleanor she hardly knew with a strength that belied her light form. They struggled and Margaret lost her footing on the stairs, tumbling down the stairs to the dungeon floor below.

When she came to, she could not see anything for the darkness. In her mouth was a cloth, secured by another around her head. Her hands and feet were tied. Her head reverberated from the thudding of her heart and she was sure she was bleeding. She felt cold and wet, as though someone had thrown a bucket of water over her. Surely she would be missed. Someone would come. Someone would find her.

Her breathing was laboured. Her muscles were in spasm and ached. She strained to hear if anyone was coming. Her tongue was dry. The cloth absorbed all the water in her mouth. She started to gag. She tried to move but in the darkness she didn't know where she was, what she would be inching towards and what she was moving away from. All she could do was make a pathetic mewling to try to attract attention.

After a long time, there was the sound of footsteps and a crackling of fire, as a torch spread its light across the dungeon. In the middle was a bloodied bundle of rags covering a lifeless form. Silence. No words were said. Then the sound of footsteps going back up the stairs. And a cry of woe for what might have been.

There have been many sightings of ghosts at Berry Pomeroy. The White Lady is often seen down in the dungeon or up on the ramparts. Sometimes she beckons to you. Sometimes she runs away. Could it be Margaret running from her sister, or is it Eleanor summoning you to witness her sister's fate?

I did a research visit to Berry Pomeroy with my Exeter Steampunk friends. As we came up out of the dungeon, a family group was in front of us with their eyes on stalks and their mouths gaping. They were not sure if we were ghosts. So if you hear any stories about a group of people rising from the dungeons in Victorian-style clothes wearing brass goggles on their top hats – you know where it came from!

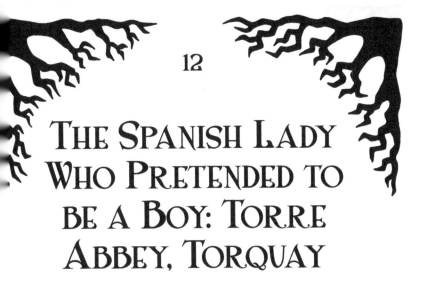

12

THE SPANISH LADY WHO PRETENDED TO BE A BOY: TORRE ABBEY, TORQUAY

I visited Torre Abbey on a bright sunny day. It's an impressive building and has a very interesting history. As you approach it there is a striking gatehouse leading to the main entrance. In your eagerness to get into the main house, it would be easy to overlook the old medieval barn that is outside. It was built for storing grain, with narrow slits for windows. Now it's been converted and is used for conferences and private functions.

Just off the entrance way to the abbey is a room that has background information on the building and especially about its role in wars from the Armada to the D-Day landings. A place that has seen much anxiety and sorrow as a backdrop to war.

On this particular day, at the far end of the gallery, there was an exhibit that was partially covered. Being nosy, we uncovered it and were surprised to see that it was R2-D2, the smaller robot from Star Wars. *We were sworn to secrecy about its presence for a wedding that was being held that afternoon. While we were exploring the upstairs rooms, we looked down from the window into the inner courtyard to see Darth Vader and six Empire soldiers, marching single file and disappearing beyond the edge of the wall. The sun was in my eyes and I thought that there was a woman in a long dress behind them, trying to keep up with them, reaching out as though to plead with them to slow down, or wait. I tried to think who she might be in* Star Wars. *She didn't have the plaits to be Princess Leia, nor the grand headdresses of Padmé, but I couldn't think who else she might be.*

We finished the tour around the house and I sat for a while to rest in the garden. I laughed as Darth Vader and the six Empire soldiers appeared again, marching through, out to the front of the house. They were obviously going to make guard of honour for the bride and groom at the end of the ceremony. I looked out for the woman, to see if I could gather any other clues about her. I couldn't see her, but I became aware of a chill. The sun's warmth no longer covered me and I thought of my fleece in the car. Behind me was the greenhouse and some gardens. I heard a sobbing. It was a woman's cry. Soft at first, then growing more intense. Whoever it was, she was clearly in distress. I looked round, but I couldn't see anyone.

I called out, 'Are you all right?' No one responded. All of a sudden there was a whoop and a cry and the bride and groom must have been making their exit. I turned aside, to go to the gate where I could watch them. The sobbing began again. If I couldn't find her, there was nothing I could do.

We watched the bride and groom step out into their new life together, under an archway of warriors of the future in this place that had such a deep connection with warriors of the past. And that's when I realised who I had heard crying.

'Will you marry me?'

The words were beyond what Luciana expected to hear.

To marry him, Mateo? She, a mere peasant girl, to marry an officer in the Spanish Armada? She knew he was fond of her and had treated her to a fine dress or two, but he was so besotted by her that now he asked her to marry him. And she was very happy to say 'Yes' to this young man that she adored, and to make her penances in the house of the Catholic God for the chance of a new life.

Just as they were married, Mateo was summoned to his ship. The King of Spain had once also been the King of England, and he had plans for his rule of the two most powerful countries and access to their treasure chests. But when his wife Queen Mary died, he was usurped by her younger sister, Elizabeth. In turn, she had changed the holy Catholic country of England into a Protestant stronghold. Her privateers threatened the Spanish dominion of the sea. A Protestant England held no joy for the King of Spain. He petitioned the Pope in Rome for permission to hold a crusade against England, to have the holy Catholic Church re-established and install a Catholic king. The Pope was more than happy to agree.

'There will be over a hundred ships,' mused Mateo. 'It will be the most miraculous sight. A Spanish Armada on a crusade to restore England to the True Church. Just as ballads and songs are written about the crusaders to Jerusalem, so shall voices be raised in our praise.'

'Will you be in danger, my amore? War is so dreadful, I cannot risk losing you.'

Mateo laughed. 'When the English hear that they have not been deserted by Rome, they will rise up, overturn their lords and ladies, the heathens will be slaughtered and a new king of the one true God will be installed to keep faith with Rome. There will be no battle. The sheer power and the authority of the King of Spain and the English people's earnest desire to return to the Catholic faith will overcome any liking for war. God is on our side. Even some of the officers' wives will be on board, that's how little danger there will be.'

As soon as the words had left his lips, he knew what her next question would be and he did not know how to answer it.

'Then may I travel with you? See what life on a ship would be like for my husband? All the better to love you and support you?' Luciana asked.

The thought of his wife on ship both thrilled him and scared him. His captain was taking his wife and there would be other women on board. Why not?

Luciana was excited and wondered how she would fare. Her husband assured her that there would be other ladies present, that she should listen to them and take instruction of how the wife of an officer should behave.

The Great and Most Fortunate Navy of Spain was due to sail from La Coruna in August 1588 under the command of the Duke of Medina Sidonia. They were to escort an army from Flanders to invade England. When Mateo reported to his ship, he was startled to find that it was carrying a large quantity of provisions. The quartermaster told him that as well as the hundred and twenty sailors and officers, they would be carrying over three hundred soldiers.

'And the wives?'

The quartermaster shot him a look. 'Not on this journey, we need the space for the soldiers. And the gunpowder.'

Mateo began to realise he had made a mistake in inviting Luciana to come on board and it was too late to make arrangements to leave her ashore. She would have to come with him. Some of the officers had cabin boys, and Mateo decided that it was better for Luciana to disguise herself as a cabin boy than compromise her reputation by being the only woman on board.

Thus it was, when the *Nuestra Senora del Rosario* left as part of the Spanish fleet, one very excited 'cabin boy' was on board watching everything.

Luciana soon found her sea legs and took this as a sign that she should be there. However, at every turn Mateo was becoming convinced that he had done the wrong thing. But he loved her so much and she loved him in turn. It was hard to hide their passion for each other, but their lives could depend upon disguising it.

As they passed Plymouth, there were shouts of English ships on the horizon, but the order was to sail on. Luciana found herself given tasks on the ship that she found physically exhausting. The men would laugh at her incompetence and Mateo did his best to keep her at his side at all times.

The sailors talked about El Draco, how the dragon had pursued other ships in the past but not this time. Perhaps the Dragon's power had flagged? Perhaps he was a Catholic and secretly hoped that the Armada would succeed in its task? The rumours and stories were rife and Luciana listened to them all in fascination.

The orders were sent between ships by pataches, small fender boats. The word came that El Draco had been spotted with his ship, the *Revenge*, and several others. The Spanish ships readied themselves for an attack.

Mateo told her, 'We fight best at close quarters. So we place ourselves to give us the greatest advantage. Stay close to the main mast and you will see us win this battle with ease.'

It was 25 July. There was an initial skirmish between the English and Spanish ships. To the Spaniards' surprise, the English ships did not come close as they usually did. This time the English ships had cannons that roared and inflicted their damage. The Spanish ships tried to get out of the way. As the *Nuestra Senora del Rosario* manoeuvred into place, another ship crashed into her, the sails caught and the halyard was damaged. The foremast came crashing down and fell on the main mast.

Luciana could see the damage. She comprehended little of what was happening, but it was obvious that *Nuestra Senora del Rosario* was seriously compromised. She now began to feel an ache in her arms and her breath became short and choppy. She found it difficult to stand and clung to the arm of Mateo. He pushed her away.

'Not now,' he said, roughly.

She watched as he called some sailors to inspect the damage with him. He was shaking his head as he spoke. A patache came from the duke asking about damage. A reply was sent by Don Pedro, the captain. No orders came, but the rest of the fleet began to progress on. The English ships seemed to pursue them, and with the breathing space the crew on the *Rosaria* tried to rationalise the damage. But as the sunset fell, they could see three English ships returning to face them.

Luciana was on deck when the English ships arrived. They kept their distance.

'See,' said Mateo, ' they are afraid to come any closer.'

There was a single voice over the water, from the English ships.

'What are they saying?' asked Luciana.

One of the sailors translated. 'He says, "I am Francis Drake, El Draco, and my matches are burning."' The cannons could be clearly seen.

Mateo now felt sick. The *Rosario* was carrying large quantities of gunpowder and with the cannon strike, they would be blown out of the water. He and his love, Luciana, and all four hundred men on board.

Luciana knew little of this. She was only aware of the desperate look in the men about her. And of the hollow, haggard look that entered Mateo's face.

Don Pedro, as captain, made his decision. He was not going to condemn the four hundred men on his ship to an explosion in the waters; he would trust that they would be captured in an honourable way and exchanged after a suitable ransom was paid. That, after all, was the rule of war. A message was sent to El Draco, to offer surrender and to ask for clemency for the crew.

Mateo thought quickly. As an officer the rules dictated that he would be kept separate from the men. But if he did that, Luciana would be left alone. He tore off his uniform and put on clothes that suggested that he was merely a sailor.

Sir Francis Drake came aboard the *Rosario*. Luciana was excited to see El Draco, this man she had heard so much about. When the captain and officers placed their swords before him, to surrender, she wondered where Mateo was. She was shocked to find him standing next to her, dressed as an ordinary sailor. He whispered that they would be prisoners together. She must not cry out or reveal herself to be a woman, because who knows what men do in the darkness of night when they believe that their God cannot see them.

As anticipated, the fifty officers were transferred to Drake's ship. A company of English sailors were stationed on board, while the *Rosario* was towed ashore. Luciana bit her lip and would not let herself descend into tears, although her whole body was shaking. She kept close to Mateo. Several of the men knew who he was and must have been puzzled as to why he would give up the status of officer with preferred quarters as his prison. And some grinned when they saw him with his cabin boy.

They were taken ashore and marched to a barn next to an abbey. We know this to be Torre Abbey, but those words meant nothing to any of those men. Three hundred people locked in a barn. No water, no food, no bedding. Mateo found a space for them beside a wall and slept between Luciana and the rest of the company. But she was fitful in the night and called out for Mateo. Around them Mateo could hear the men were also restless. No words of comfort could be said in private.

When the sun rose some of the sailors began banging on the doors pleading to be let out for latrines, or water, or out of that foul air of the night. Looking through one of the slanted windows, Mateo could see that mounted lancers had been placed around the barn to guard them. Two men on horses were arguing. Mateo could just about understand them.

'Who is to pay for guarding them? For feeding them?'

'The Privy Council will pay.'

'I'll not spend a penny until I get some money in advance.'

And with that one of the men turned his horse and rode off, while the other shook his head.

Mateo's heart sank. Maybe he should have gone with the other officers – at least no one would query how they were to be fed and watered. He realised that just by being corralled in the barn with three hundred people, he was already thinking of himself as a caged animal, not a man. And what about Luciana?

Her belly ached and rumbled and her mouth felt like thin paper. Sleeping on the ground had chilled her and yet the heat from three hundred men packed into the barn overwhelmed her. A July night in England was not the same as in Spain. She realised full well that her situation was dire. Should she declare herself a woman and try to get herself out of there? But then she would be leaving Mateo behind, and he had already given up his role as officer to be with her. What dangers would she face with English soldiers? It had all seemed so romantic and now the fairy tale was turning into a nightmare.

It wasn't until past noon that a barrel of water was rolled into the barn. The doors were unlocked and there was a skirmish to get the ladles to drink the water. Luciana was next to the barrel when the lid was taken off and on instinct she thrust her head under the water and drank in as much as she could, until she felt a hand at the back of her head pushing her down. She struggled, but her hands slipped and she had nothing to brace herself. The breath escaped her body and in a moment she wondered if her soul too would take its leave. As she felt her body go limp she was pulled up into the air and thrown on the ground.

'Don't let your cabin boy try that one again, else he'll get nothing!'

Luciana gasped for air and wiped the water from her face. Mateo was on the ground, his face bruised and bloodied. One of the sailors was standing over him, with his red fists clenched.

'Sorry. Sorry,' she whispered. 'Sorry.'

There was no food for three days. Nothing at all. The water was rationed and a great show was made of Mateo and Luciana having the last drops. Luciana withdrew into herself, sitting on the floor, her arms wrapped around her legs and rocking back and forth. Mateo found her a corner of the barn near one of the window slits and tried to keep the other prisoners away from her. But they did not want to know. They could see she already had the prison madness. They had their own problems. With no latrines the ground was covered in faeces and urine. And vomit, for a fever was rife among the prisoners.

On the fourth day an English soldier came into the barn and began dividing them into two groups. One group to remain in the barn, the other to go outside.

Mateo was directed to go in the second group. He turned and went to support Luciana, to bring her too, but the English soldier thrust his musket into Mateo's back, then kicked him when he fell to the ground.

'Out!' said the English soldier. 'Out!'

Luciana barely comprehended what was happening and staggered to her feet as Mateo was dragged away, unconscious.

'No, no, no!' she cried. She took one step, then another. 'No!'

Then she fell to the ground.

In her bewildered state she was hardly aware as half the prisoners were taken out and then marched away. The ones who were left were those who were ill or not able to walk. The doors closed on them again.

'Mateo!' Luciana croaked.

Without him to support her, she knew she would not last long. She had no strength even to get to the water barrel. One of the other prisoners took pity on her and brought her a cup, but her lips were already cracked and her throat so rasped with thirst that the few drops left for her were agonising as she drank them down.

With half the company gone, there was at least more space and no one fought Luciana for her corner. She sat and rocked, with her head in a fever, and dreamed.

Here she was at the church with Mateo. The best day of her life. He in his uniform, she in her simple linen dress. In her hands there was a bouquet. He knew she was from peasant stock, but he didn't mind. He loved her. After the church, they walked up the hill, to the place where they first met. And there they sealed the bond of their marriage. There would be one, two, three children – maybe more. The first two would be sons for Mateo. They would go to sea, like their father. But the third would be a girl for her and she would never go to sea. Mateo and she would live long lives and die in each other's arms, surrounded by their loving children.

The doors of the barn creaked as they were pulled open. Another water barrel was rolled in and set up. Alongside it were placed some baskets with bread and fish that had seen better days. The prisoners descended on the food and fights broke out between them while they each tried to grab as much as possible. In her corner Luciana made no attempt to get up, to fend for herself. In her fever she was in a different world.

Mateo! Mateo my love, it is supper time! Where are you my dear love. Don't hide from me. Is this a game, that you want me to come looking for you? Come out now my love. Where are you?

They left her in the corner as she moved her cracked lips, whispering wordlessly.

No one took her water. No one took her any of the rancid food.

When finally the English deigned to allow the prisoners out to exercise and experience the sun, Luciana had died.

The abandonment of the Rosario *by the Spanish Armada led to disillusionment within the Spanish rank and file and a breaking of the trusted bond of not being left behind. They knew now they were all open to being sacrificed.*

The officers were ransomed a year later and returned to their homes.

The English had made no provision for prisoners and no budgets for their care. Consequently payment for their keep was an ongoing battle between the Privy Council, who wanted to pay in arrears, and the local landed gentry, Cary and Gilbert, who had been tasked to keep the prisoners and wanted to be paid in advance. The fact that the Rosario held enough provisions was not considered until it was too late and by that time the 2,000 litres of red wine that she carried had already been relieved from the ship.

Mateo and the other men were marched off to the prison at Brixham, where Cary relented and paid for their provisions.

In the barn, those prisoners that did not die were forced to work on Gilbert's farm, to bring in the harvest.

And Luciana? It is said that the ghost of a Spanish lady haunts the barn and the grounds of Torre Abbey, seeking her true love. Maybe there was an unexpected guest at that wedding? Maybe there was someone who had come dressed as a female warrior?

Or maybe it was just a reflection in the sun.

13

A Father's Love: Dartmouth

As you stand in Dartmouth, with your back to the sea, look up into the hills. There you can see the Naval College. Before this fine building was built, there was one that was much grander: a mansion that was the pride and delight of Squire Boone. He had done very well for himself in business and his house reflected his success and wealth.

He adored his daughter Mary, his sole heiress and his pride and joy. Her mother had died when she was born, as often happened in that time. He had devoted himself to her, making sure she had a fine education, and he loved his daughter dearly. Whenever he had to travel he encouraged her to accompany him; and when it was not appropriate for Mary to go with him, he wrote to her every day. He brought back the finest silks and satins for her and delighted in seeing his daughter dressed in the height of fashion. He took her to the local balls and watched as Mary danced with the fine young gentlemen. The old ladies and his colleagues commented favourably on her fine taste and delicate movement in the dances. Mary always made sure that her father had his share of dances too, and he was aware of the glances of envy from the men young and old.

But it is the way of life that presenting a young woman at social gatherings will have consequences of a romantic kind. Several young men asked for permission to call upon Mary and it was with a dawning sense of despair that he realised they planned to court her, with a view to marriage. She was a fine catch, no doubt about that. His prosperity had come at a personal cost and now he could afford to bask in the glory of his position, but he had a dilemma. He had hoped that his daughter would make a good match, possibly with someone with an aristocratic connection to bring a touch of glamour to his family name. But was it possible he might lose Mary to some love-struck swain who would only be after his money?

He could not contemplate losing his daughter; his companion, confidante and cherished support. He realised that he envisaged a long life with his daughter by his side, supporting him and caring for him as he had hoped her mother would. If Mary married she might move away, never to see him again, or worse, die in childbirth as her mother had.

He refused to allow any young men entry to the house. All invitations to balls, afternoon teas, visits to pleasure gardens and other social gatherings were declined. Mary was distraught. Having become accustomed to being a social success and in demand, she was now bereft of company. She pleaded and begged with her father to allow her to attend something. He was adamant that she should not leave the house except in his company and he would supervise any social interaction.

He did suggest, however, that maybe he could invite some of his colleagues and their wives for an afternoon of cards and conversation. Mary's relief at having some diversion was palpable.

'Thank you, father. It would a great pleasure to entertain your friends.'

It was the gossip of the town, how Squire Boone had withdrawn his daughter from society. When it became known that he would only allow his daughter to entertain at home with his friends, remarkably there was some jockeying for position. After all, there are mothers whose interest it was to acquire their younger sons a favourable match, allowing the older ones to attract the attention of the heiresses with their own fortunes and titles.

So while Squire Boone drank and conversed with his companions, the ladies had a different kind of discussion. Advice was given; after all, this was a young woman whose mother had died and who knew nothing of the realities of married love. Mary listened avidly and learned well what she must look for in a young man and hints of what a marriage would bring. It was pleasing when some of the women privately advocated their

own sons, reminding Mary of the social occasions when she had met them and the particulars of what they looked like so that she could form an image of them. Some even produced miniature portraits to encourage her.

Squire Boone was ignorant of all this. He congratulated himself on having the perfect solution, whereby Mary was presented as his companion in a company of equals. His daughter did not need more than this.

Mary was playing the long game. At the first ball she had attended she met a young man, Teddie, with whom she wanted to form a liaison. His letters to her were carried in the butcher-boy's apron and relayed to her by one of the servants. As the cards and conversation became a regular pattern in their lives, she encouraged her father to vary the guests, until at last he invited the mother of her lover. The lady in question was delighted to act as go-between and even to contribute to the plot for an elopement.

A date was agreed. Mary's bags were packed. Her servant had removed them to the pantry and all that was needed was for Mary to leave the house at the designated hour.

All would have been well, if it had not been for Squire Boone's sleeplessness. For some time it had been his habit to read in the library with a glass of whisky until he became so tired that he would make his way to bed. Mary had become so infatuated with her pending elopement that she had not noticed her father's indisposition or preference for remedy. As she came down the stairs in the darkness, she held her shoes in one hand and lifted the skirt in the other. But skirts, without shoes, gain an inch or two. Unaccustomed to the extra length, she caught her right toe in the front hem of her skirt and tumbled down the remaining three steps to the hall, in front of the quaking servant girl who held her bags.

Her father came storming out of the library, candle in hand. He put the candle down on a side table, grabbed his daughter by her arms and hauled her to her feet. Mary watched her father's face as it was full of concern for her. Then in an instant he drew a sharp breath in, his lips tightened into a straight line, eyes bulged and the veins in his neck stood out. The howl that came from his mouth would have woken the Devil himself. The candle flickered and Mary could not be sure whether the shadows showed her father with horns.

Squire Boone fell to his knees on the tiled floor and begged his daughter to stay. With tears flowing he spoke of his love for her mother, his fears of being left alone, of the joy that she brought to him in this life and the despair and loneliness that would engulf him should she leave, which would only drive him to join her mother in her grave.

Distraught beyond words at the grief she had caused her father, she knelt down beside him and promised – vowed – gave him her word – she would never leave him, that she would give up the young man straight away and never look at another. Her father was everything to her and she begged for his forgiveness at being such a foolish daughter.

The servant was sent to tell the young man to leave without her. His cries and banging on the front door echoed around the stairwell, as Mary accompanied her father upstairs. Two men sobbed for Mary that night, but it was only her father that she could give her attention to.

In the following months and years, the house was quiet. No more cards and conversation. The servants who had assisted her had been dismissed and Mary no longer had any allies about her. She was restless and dearly wanted to go out of the house. Her father, caught in the trauma and shock of his daughter's potential departure, became suspicious. The servants were checked, asked about her every move. He became uncertain of everyone, afraid even to eat. His cheekbones protruded as he asked again and again that Mary not leave him and she promised again and again that she never would. She swore that all contact between her and her lover was forsaken. He was her father and eternal companion and she was faithful only to him.

Squire Boone, caught up in the hindrances of keeping his daughter in his solitary tower, became ill and slowly deteriorated. Mary was indeed the faithful daughter, encouraging him to eat, and as she brought the spoon to his mouth with the broth, he would grab her arm as he had done in the hall on that night and say, 'Don't leave me. Please don't leave me.'

It was Squire Boone who finally left. On a cold wet February day he breathed his last. Mary wept for him. There was a funeral and all the cards and conversation guests came to pay their last respects – along with a few of their sons, who saw an opportunity.

Teddie had never given up hope. As Mary's father was lowered into the ground, he stood by Mary and slipped his hand over hers. A gesture that showed respect for the honour she did her father, but which also told her that now was her time.

She waited six months past her father's death and then invited Teddie and his mother to afternoon tea. The wedding was soon arranged and the bouquet was thrown from the top of the stairs which she had so carefully crept down all those years before.

Her father's room was kept as he had left it. He would not be disturbed.

As Teddie led her up to the bedroom they would share, both anticipated their new lives and hopes for family. Mary was filled with passion for Teddie as he kissed her, unchaperoned for the first time. As she did so, there was a clattering noise and some books fell from the shelf. As they kissed again, the window frames rattled and flew open, the curtains billowing inside. Teddie crossed the room to close the window, but something rolled in front of him and he tripped over it. It was a glass that shattered on impact and cut his hand. Some considerable time was spent administering to his wound. The lovers retired to their beds, their passion unrequited.

In the morning they decided to refashion the house in their own way. Tables were moved, vases repositioned as they explored the potential. But Mary was confused. Why did they always appear back in their original places? Thinking at first it was Teddie playing tricks on her, she challenged him. He, of course, denied it – how would he know what the original placements were? It was all new to him. The servants denied anything too. They were also new to the house, having replaced her father's conspirators.

That evening they were both in the library before retiring to their unconsummated marital bed. Teddie had moved the big leather armchair closer to the fire while he supped his glass of port. He got up to replenish his glass and heard Mary's gasp. He turned round to see his chair gliding over the carpet to its original position. By itself. He heard a chink and looked down to see the port decanter move across the table, with the stopper firmly back in place. Mary's eyes were wide. Her lips were quivering. Shaking her head, she cried 'No, no, no!' and fled the room, Teddie following her. In the hall the candles were flickering. Mary screamed. Teddie watched as she seemed to be pulled by her upper arms across the room.

'Let go of me. Dear God, let go!' she cried. She stopped abruptly, as though something had released her. The candles went out. Mary gave a great howl.

Somehow Teddie got her back to their room, the fire burning in the grate. Mary made him put something before the door, even though both of them knew it would make no difference. They were still awake in the morning as the sun came up. On her arms huge bruises had developed.

'I don't want to speak about this. But I want to leave now!' she said.

They packed a bag each, arranged for the house to be shut down and Teddie sent for a carriage to take them to London.

'As far away as possible!' she wept.

Teddie had friends in London and at first they stayed with them. But tensions grew between them. Mary was afraid that her father's ghost was watching her and that God himself was observing her actions. She was unable to seal the contract between husband and wife. Teddie decided that they needed space for themselves with no associations with family and friends. He found a small house, suited to their needs. In the quiet of the house they shared tender moments, until Mary felt safe enough to enjoy her marital status. On one sunny afternoon, when the servants had been dismissed, they lay in each other's arms reaching for that embrace ... CRASH!

Every piece of china in the house was broken. Plates, bowls, cups, saucers, teapots and chocolate pots, figurines and even small statues.

Mary had had enough. 'He follows me even here. Let us go home and call him to rights.'

The journey was in silence. Teddie was at a loss to know what to do or say. He reached out his hand to comfort her, but she pulled away from him, frightened at what might happen next.

The house had been opened up and two bedrooms made up: one for Mary and one for Teddie. Mary spent the night in fear that her father might still seek retribution on her. Teddie could only think of his wife, how dearly he loved her, but how long could their marriage last under such pressure?

The local bishop was informed of the situation. He and some of his clergy attended the following afternoon. Only one of them had carried out an exorcism before. It was decided that the hallway at the foot of the stairs was the best place to perform the ceremony and chairs were placed so that all might sit.

The incantations, the incenses and the holy water were spread and distributed. The hall clock began to chime loudly, and then rocked as if it were to fall. Ornaments and pictures clattered and swayed in their places; some tumbled to the ground. The prayers continued.

Finally an outline appeared – fading in and out of strength. Soon it was recognisable as Squire Boone. Mary's hands lifted to her mouth.

'Father, why have you done this to me?'

Squire Boone stood before her, incandescent in his spiritual form.

'I want only to protect you,' he said. 'My beautiful daughter. My pride and joy.'

'Father,' she said, 'you do not protect me. You make my life a misery. I have no pride as I hide from my husband, I have no joy from being wed. I am alone and it is all because of you. I beg you, let me live my own life without you. Your memory is with me always, I will always love you, but that love is of the past. I have a love of the future, to find the new adventures our family will have and I want to face them with Teddie. My husband. My lover. And despite all your machinations I will have a child and your grandchild will come into this world with a family that wishes to honour your name. Please leave us.'

The clergy watched all this. They continued with their prayers and incantations.

'I want nothing more than the best for you. I will leave you here on this earth, if you promise to join me in the afterlife when the time comes,' the ghost of Squire Boone begged his daughter.

'Father, I do not know what happens in the afterlife and cannot commit myself until I know what my life here will be.'

The bishop stepped forward.

'Be gone, man, take Christ's redemption in the house of your father and let the living praise those of this world, so that the other world will be assured of eternal salvation.'

With that, the bishop threw the remaining holy water on the shadow of Squire Boone.

Everything stopped. Nothing moved. Not even the clock ticking.

'He's gone,' sighed Mary.

Restored to peace and calm, Mary and Teddie were able to be the husband and wife they aspired to be. Mary was thrilled when she learned of her forthcoming child and they made great plans.

They spoke often of her father and hoped that his spirit was with them in the joy of the new child. At her confinement she asked for the same doctor who had attended her mother.

Teddie was pacing up and down, supping his whisky. His best friends were in the library playing cards while they waited to hear the news. There was a bellowing from upstairs, cries of 'Father!' then silence. A loud gasp and a thin wailing.

The doctor came down with a bundle in his arms.

'Here is your daughter. Bless her and give her joy. But with sadness I must tell you her mother is dead. Died in childbirth, as her mother did before her. I tended her mother then and was distraught at having lost her, but my father told me that even her grandmother died in the same way. I fear this small one may in time suffer the same fate. So cherish her and keep her close.'

From the corner of his eye Teddie saw a shimmering shadow with tears streaming down its ghostly visage. And now he understood what he had to do as a father.

Some people say that Squire Boone still haunts the grounds of Dartmouth College, sometimes on foot, or sometimes on a horse. His daughter is nowhere to be seen.

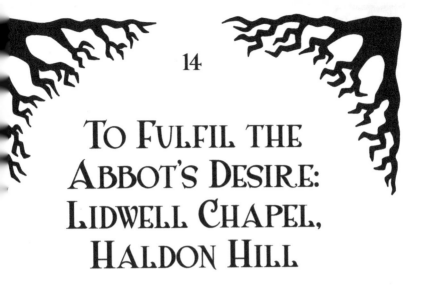

14

To Fulfil the Abbot's Desire: Lidwell Chapel, Haldon Hill

If you go to Lidwell, just outside Teignmouth, no matter what time of year, be sure to take a pair of wellington boots. There you will find the ruins of an old chapel. Not much of it is left now and it is all fenced off. But just inside the fence is a well that seems to be flooding the area. This is Our Lady's Well, from which the name Lidwell is derived.

Robert de Middlecote was a dedicated man of God and faithful to his brethren and their monastic order. He had spent ten years at a chapel in Cornwall. There he had struggled to learn the Cornish language and trusted in God that this trial was his destiny in life. He had a responsibility to his abbot to raise money for the main abbey, as well as distributing money locally to ensure the well-being of the spiritual life of the community he served. But the men of Cornwall were difficult, corrupt and somehow brought a malign influence to his house. This was something that Robert did not quite understand and it made him uncomfortable.

For a long time there was very little money sent to the abbey but then there came a regular trickle. Two monks were sent to investigate and congratulate Robert for his achievements, but what they found horrified them and they scurried back to the abbey and informed the abbot.

The decision was quickly made that as a 'reward' for his efforts in Cornwall, Robert was transferred to Lidwell Chapel, a remote place in Devon which was little visited, but closer to the abbey. A good place for someone whose working life had been very, shall we say, eventful.

And there Robert found the peace and quiet that he needed to rest, reflect and give praise to God. He no longer had the responsibility to raise money or distribute any to the community. But somehow, that old imperative that had been so heavily engrained

into him haunted him in those early hours of the morning when he was at prayer. That defensive shield he had crafted to protect him from malign influences came back.

He became anxious, waiting for the day when the abbot would berate him for not collecting the monies that the abbey would need. In his confusion, he antici-pated the day his brothers would return to demand the sum and he had none to offer, none to deliver, none to give to the glory of God. A man sequestered away from his brethren, alone and with no reassurances, will soon fall into a fool's paranoia and he determined that it was the will of God that he should prepare himself for that day.

At first Robert was able to put all dark thoughts from him. During the spring he spent his days wandering across the Haldon Forest ways and hills, so that he felt he knew every tree, every blade of grass. Sometimes he would meet travellers who were not sure of the path through the woods. He would offer to show them and as he was a man of the cloth, they gave their trust and thanks, allowing him to guide them. Sometimes, if they were passing by the chapel, he would invite them in to take some refreshment, food and maybe a little rest, a blessing and some guidance to find their own path. Word soon spread of the monk at Lidwell Chapel who was so kind and accommodating. Travellers felt encouraged to seek him out.

For as long as the sun was high in the sky, all was well. But it was when it began its return to the dark side earlier and earlier each day that Robert became more anxious. Travellers would risk the journey to the chapel to stay the night, because they knew they would get a warm and safe welcome.

The sun had just gone down one day when there was a knock on the chapel door. Two men stood there.

'Good even to you, Father. We have journeyed this day and are in need of rest and sustenance. We had hoped to make it over the hills this evening but we've been delayed. May we shelter here and leave in the morning?'

The second one joined in. 'And we can give offerings for our night's stay.'

Robert waved them in and they sat at his table. He had very simple fare for them, only bread and cheese, but they were grateful to have something. Robert offered them a drink of his own wine and they were glad to raise their tankards. They did not seem suspicious when they both became rapidly sleepy and made their way to the rough bed that was on offer to them.

That was when Robert took their bags and rummaged through them. As he suspected, they were two merchants travelling in disguise with a goodly pouch of gold on them. Robert was reassured. God had sent them his way and now he could start collecting what was due to Him.

He was not a man to take a knife to another but the two men had to be disposed of. Lighting another candle, he took it into the chapel and wedged it in a nook in the wall. He went back to his room and one by one, he dragged them in.

In the corner of the chapel was Our Lady's Well. With a struggle Robert got the two of them to the lip of the well and then threw them in one at a time. The well was quite deep. The bodies clattered against the stone walls as they tumbled down and then splashed at the bottom. One must have been supported by the other above the water level, because Robert could hear a slight groaning. The sleeping potion in the beer had begun to wear off and at least one of them was injured and awake. Robert put his hands over his ears, turned to the altar and then began singing praises to God.

It might have been two or maybe three hours later that Robert stopped his chant. He took his hands from his ears and held them out either side of himself. The candle he brought in earlier was guttering. All he could hear now was the owls calling in the fields. His work was done.

The pouch of gold needed to be secured. Kept safe. Robert knew now that there would be other opportunities. He needed to be ready.

He asked the local carpenter for wood to make an altar for the chapel. The carpenter offered to make one himself, but Robert insisted that it had to be made by a holy man and that he had some skill in this work. When the altar was finished, it was rough and ready but at its heart was a secret chamber to which only Robert had access.

The gold was placed in the box.

The second time Robert had an affluent-looking guest, he invited them into the chapel itself, so that he might offer a blessing and a communion to wish the traveller well. As the unsuspecting stranger closed his eyes, then lifted the goblet to drink, his throat was exposed and Robert slashed it with his knife. Then only a few paces to the well and throw him down. Much more efficient. Not so far to drag the body and no cries if the fall hadn't already proved fatal.

The villagers appreciated the time and care the monk was paying to the chapel and donated candles, candlesticks and cloth. One offered two pewter tankards for communion, a blanket for his bed and hay for his bedframe. Some came to spend the time of day with him but they all knew that the time to leave was well before sunset, when he became very restless and sometimes rude. However, they knew he had other tasks to do in God's name and they were not privy to the monk's rites.

Robert was busy during the day, giving comfort and succour to those travelling and guiding them through the forest. Where they gave him a few coins to thank him and God for his help, he would say a prayer and a blessing. But always in the back of his mind he would be preparing for the day when the abbot would want his reckoning.

His night-time exploits brought him a good bounty, always hidden in the altar. Sometimes he would sit next to the open chamber in the altar and, by the light of the flickering candle, he would count the money and know that the abbot would be pleased.

For several years Robert managed to get away with his deeds. The abbot had long dismissed him as an irrelevance but Robert did not know this. However, it is one of those conundrums of life that sometimes you lose track of your original purpose. The pleasure of service was overtaken by the pleasure of committing the deed. Robert was no longer selective about whose throat he might now cut or whose life he might take, or even how much gold would be added to the abbot's pot. Now it was the challenge of finding a victim, enticing them to the chapel and then the sense of power he had in deciding whether he would he let them live or die. If they had money or treasure to go into the altar, his altar, then all the better.

In all this time no one knew, no one suspected the kindly monk who went out of his way to look after lost travellers. Because once they were through the forest, anything could happen to them, couldn't it?

One day a lieutenant in the navy was on his way home and came by the chapel. Robert welcomed him in and, looking at the sun sliding down, invited him to take a blessing and communion then share a meal before bedding down. The sailor was thankful for the offer and so he followed Robert into the chapel where the candles were already alight on the walls.

The lieutenant knelt before the altar as many had done before him. The words of the service were said. The goblet of wine was raised to his lips. His eyes, as ritual demanded, were closed. Then one of the candles spluttered and cracked. In that moment the sailor's eyes opened and he could see the knife heading for his throat. With a lifetime of battles on street and ship, the sailor fell to one side, then leaped to his feet to grab the knife. Robert was unprepared for his actions, stood up and staggered back. The sailor reached out for Robert's knife hand and Robert began to retreat, slashing at him, catching his hand. They began to circle each other when the sailor decided to rush at Robert to put him off balance and make him drop the knife. In the dim light Robert did not realise how close he was to the well. One backwards step and he tumbled in, giving a great cry. As he fell down all he could see was the outline of the head of the sailor, backlit by the candles. The only thought in his head was to wonder if each of his victims had seen him in such a way too.

Crack! One of Robert's bones was broken. But he was alive to feel the pain.

'Have pity on me,' he cried, 'I am but one of God's servants. Get me out of here.'

The lieutenant knelt on the floor by the well. 'The Devil, more like!' he cried.

He had more humanity in him than that miscreant down the well. It was too dark to go out into the woods – he had no idea where he was – so he slept on the monk's bed and went back to the well at the first light of day.

'Hey, you!'

Robert was awake, still part in delirium and in much pain. 'For the love of God, get me out of here.'

The sailor paused at the door of the chapel, looked first to where the path led away through the forest and then back towards the farm he knew he had seen two miles west the day before. He shook his head and then started running towards the farmhouse.

The farmer was shocked to see a man bloodied and out of breath, banging on his farmhouse door before he had even milked the cows. The man made no sense but all he could hear was that the monk had fallen down the well and needed help. Looking at the blood on the man's clothes, the farmer called his sons to come with him just in case this was the wrongdoer here.

The farmer had a soft spot for the monk and he hoped that nothing bad had happened. His sons brought the ropes and the four of them made their way up to the chapel. The farmer tried to piece together what had happened but the man sounded drunk, accusing the holy father of trying to kill him.

When they arrived at the chapel, there were signs of a fight there.

The farmer called down the well and was relieved to hear a voice back that he knew was Father Robert. Both of Robert's arms had been broken, so one of the farmer's sons was lowered down to put the ropes under the monk's arms. He had with him a flaming torch and when he arrived at the bottom, he wedged it between two stones so that he could see what he was doing. Praising the Lord that the well wasn't too deep, the young man did what he could then called to his father to raise Robert. The farmer turned to the sailor to give him an end of the rope. For a second the sailor hesitated and then reached for it.

They hauled Robert up out of the well and he collapsed into the arms of the other young son, who gently and reverently lowered him to the floor. Loosening the ropes, the farmer started lowering them down the well to his other son. He could see the light moving about below and knew his boy was well.

There came a scream from the bottom of the well. 'Get me out of here, get me out of here.'

As they pulled the lad up, they could hear him shouting, 'Get off me. Get off me!'

He was swinging on the rope so much it was difficult for the farmer and the sailor to pull him up.

'Stay still, lad, or you'll fall back down again.'

There was a whimpering and then the rapid movement slowed, with just a small jerking.

The young man was at the top and grabbed at his father's arm.

'Don't let them take me. For God's sake, don't let them take me.'

As he was lifted out, his father could see what was causing his distress. Caught around his leg was the rotting skeleton of a child.

Behind them, Robert gave a wail to his Almighty, the broken bones of his arms projecting out of his monk's clothing. 'I didn't mean to take the child. But his mother wore such a beautiful necklace.'

Robert was taken back to the monastery, where they tended to his broken arms and kept him under observation. The monks were under a vow of silence about what had previously happened in Cornwall, but they all knew.

They went down the well to see if there were any more bodies. There were many: where the water had come into the well there was an underwater cave and the bones had silted up against that.

The bodies were raised up for burial but no man could stomach the task for long. It took several hours.

The sailor was originally charged with some of the murders. No one believed that Robert was responsible but the number of bodies showed that it was done over a long time. In the process of laying out the bodies, the altar was moved and in doing so the treasure was found. The sailor was exonerated from any charge and allowed to go on his way.

Robert was taken from his monk's cell and executed on the gallows in 1329.

Some people say that on a wild and gusty night, the ghost of Robert can be seen in the chapel standing over the well, or counting his treasure in the altar. Some say his ghost can be seen wandering Haldon Forest, looking for travellers to offer his own kind of hospitality. And some tell their children that if they do not behave they will get a visit from the monk of Lidwell.

15

FOLLOWING THE OLD CORPSE ROAD: AXMINSTER

'How much longer must we carry this coffin?' called out Davy. 'It will be getting dark soon and I don't hold with carrying dead folk after the sun has gone down.'

It had been a long day. The coffin had lain on the shoulders of the four men for most of the past three hours.

'Probably another hour before we get to Axminster, then we can break for the night,' replied John. 'There's a coffin stone up ahead, we can place it there, while we take a rest.'

Michael and Samuel just grunted in agreement. It was a heavy responsibility that had been laid on their shoulders, literally.

They had been summoned by the parish priest to the farmhouse that offered accommodation to travellers. On the hall floor, next to the bottom of the staircase, was a man's body. Kneeling over it was the doctor, shaking his head. The farmer was standing next to the doctor, with his son by him, trembling. The parish priest had his arm on the farmer's son's shoulder.

'It's all right, Jamie,' said the priest. 'It will be all right.'

'Definitely dead. Drunk too, you can smell the whisky on him.' The doctor looked up at the parish priest and the farmer. 'I'll sign the papers. There is nothing suspicious about this. He must have drunk too much last night. When he woke he was disorientated and fell down the staircase. He must have hit his head as he fell. Not your fault. Nothing to worry about.'

The farmer nodded his head. The priest patted Jamie's shoulder reassuringly. From upstairs a cry was heard, perhaps from a woman? But no one appeared.

'He'll need some kind of shroud. Do you have anything? And someone to wind him into it?' asked the doctor.

Jamie became animated. 'We have something we can use. And I'll wind him.' The tone of his voice was quite sharp. He was no longer trembling.

'You say he comes from Exeter? What's his name?' said the doctor as he turned to the farmer. Another cry from upstairs, stifled.

'Yes, he said he was a merchant there,' replied the farmer. 'His name's Jeremy Tyler. He had some business over this way and he was travelling homewards. He was staying here just the night. I guess his business was successful and he took to his cups to celebrate!'

The priest muttered his agreement.

'And the last rites?' asked the doctor.

'He was dead before I got here,' said the priest, 'but I have said the prayers for his soul.'

'What shall we do with the body?' asked the farmer. 'He will have to go back to Exeter, he will have family there. But there is no money for a carriage to take him all the way there and I fear if I pay myself, that I may never see it back again. If we sell his horse there is enough for these boys to carry him in a box on the old corpse road to Axminster and then for him to be taken in a cart to Exeter.'

'Why the old corpse road?' asked the doctor. It seemed to him that it had been a long time since it had last been used.

John spoke up. 'If we are to carry him, it's quicker and easier over the old way. Otherwise we have to carry him on the main road and have all sorts of boundaries to cross. If we have to cross the tolls and fences then the soul cannot pass that way and becomes lost and may come back to haunt them here.'

The doctor look a little amused at some of the old ways.

'I don't want his soul coming back here to haunt us,' said the farmer. 'I want him to cross water so that his soul is kept far enough away. The boys know the path, they know the rivers to cross and they know how to confound his soul so that it never comes back.'

The doctor looked at the farmer. He was surprised at the venom in the farmer's voice. The farmer's son saw the look and intervened.

'It's my sister. She found the body and now she is fearful that he will return to haunt her. We have told her that there is no reason for him to do that, but she's a God-fearing woman and very sensitive. We want to do the right thing for her.'

The doctor nodded. He had seen this before and appreciated the effort the men were trying to make to reduce the risk of hysterics in the woman.

'Very well,' he said. 'Jamie, you wind the body in the shroud and you men bring the coffin. I'll sign the papers.' He turned to the farmer. 'And you'll write to the family to expect his body?'

The farmer looked sheepish. 'My hand is not so good for writing. Would you do that?'

The doctor sighed. 'Yes, give me the address.'

The coffin stone was not too far ahead and they lowered their burden onto it.

Davey asked, 'Why did we have to wait until we reached these stones? Couldn't we put the coffin on the ground a while back?'

John laughed. 'You youngsters know nothing. If we place the coffin on the ground, then the soul can run free from the body. You see, the soul stays with the body until it gets to its final resting place in consecrated ground, so long as there are no man-made boundaries to hold them back. That's why we pick our way across the moors. No old walls, no fences, nothing to cause the soul to leave the body. But once they've gone over a natural boundary like water, they cannot cross back. You heard the farmer – they don't want this man's soul to come back and haunt them.'

'How many times did we cross water? I never knew there was so many waterways!' asked Davey, his interest piqued.

Michael cuffed him. 'Too many questions! Just know that we've made sure that his soul will never make its way back to that farmhouse. Now come on, one last shift and we'll be in Axminster! We'll settle at the Green Dragon inn. My cousin told me about it – they'll look after us.'

They reached the inn just as the sun went down. The four men stood with the coffin on their shoulders, fearful to lay it on the ground. Michael sent for the landlord and explained that they need to rest both themselves and the coffin.

'You've come along the corpse road? Following the old ways?' asked the landlord. 'Then best you place the coffin in the stable. There are some blocks in there you can rest it on, that should be distance enough from the ground for you. Leave it there and come in to tell me the story!'

And so the coffin was laid down.

'Has he gone?' The farmer's daughter was distraught. 'Father! You're sure he's not coming back?'

The farmer held her tight. 'No, he's not coming back. Jamie made sure of that.'

Jamie nodded. 'After that blow you gave him with the rolling pin, he wasn't going to wake up too soon. The doctor was sure he was dead.'

'He came at me from behind. I didn't hear him and then he was all over me. I grabbed the first thing to hand.' She cried, tears running down her face.

The farmer patted her back reassuringly. 'You did well lass. You did well.' He looked at Jamie. 'Smart move that was, pouring some of my whisky in his throat and putting him at the bottom of the stairs. The doctor was easily befuddled.'

'But you're sure he's dead?' she asked again.

'I put the shroud on him myself. Finished it with a knot tight around his neck and his ankles. And a few other touches. If he is not dead already, he soon will be,' replied Jamie. 'And the lads know the moors. You'll be fine. He won't be back to haunt you, living or dead.'

As Jeremy Tyler came to, he had such a pain in his head. It was dark; he couldn't imagine where he was. He tried to put a hand to his head but something restrained his arms. He thought he was blind – there was only darkness and it felt like there was a hood over his head. He tried to sit up but he raised only a few inches before his forehead hit something and he fell back.

He blinked rapidly but could not see anything. He listened but there was silence and only the beating of his heart in his ear. He tried to swallow but some cloth had been rammed in his mouth. He could feel his Adam's apple moved up and down but it was constrained. His nostrils swelled with the smell of urine. It made him retch, but as his throat spasmed he lost the little air that was available to him. His torso began to contort instinctively as he tried to gain control over his bodily functions, but too late. The liquid seeped between his legs and he could feel the warmth as it was absorbed by this shroud.

Where was he? His greatest fear was that he was in a coffin already placed under the ground. How long could he survive? He tried to kick, make a noise by raising his legs as a little as he could and then swinging them against the side of the box. *Call it a box. Not a coffin.* He listened to the sound that it made. He was certain that if he was underground, then the sound would be muffled. But it wasn't. It was a noise with an echo. He tried and tried again, raising his legs and trying to hit the sides. The result was a struggle to breathe and an exhaustion that swept over him.

He wasn't sure if he had drifted in and out of sleep but he could hear singing. He definitely could hear singing. *Angels? Could they be angels?* Through the surface of the box he could hear something above him, several thuds, a cry or two and then a rasping noise. Jeremy could feel the tears streaming down his face. Someone had fallen asleep on the coffin. This could be his salvation. With all his might he raised himself, twisted and turned, trying to make a noise with any part of his body that could make contact with the inside of the box.

Michael was keen to be up early and secure passage for the coffin to Exeter. With the balance of the money from the sale of the horse, he found someone who was prepared to take the coffin and the letter to Exeter on a donkey cart. He went back to the

Green Dragon inn. The four men lifted the coffin onto the cart and watched it taken away, over the River Axe.

'A good job well done, lads,' said John. 'Good riddance to him. Now home again.' The four men walked away, back to whence they had come.

At the Green Dragon, the ostler was being teased. The night before he had drunk a little too much and he had been turned out of the room he had shared with the servants.

'And where did you sleep last night? What was her name?' they laughed.

'Just by my lonesome!' he laughed in return. 'And the stable was fine enough for me. Dry and warm. I slept on an old box in there and pulled a sack over my head.' He paused. 'Mind you, those rats are damned noisy. All night long I could hear them scrabbling as if they were trying to get into the stable.'

His fellow servants stopped and looked at him.

'What's the matter?' he guffawed. 'Scared of a few large rats are you?' Now he had the laugh on them.

'If you were in the stables,' queried the barman, 'did you not see the coffin lying there? Because I don't recall there being any other box there?'

'A coffin?' The ostler stood up. 'My God. The scratching and thumping sounds underneath me. Someone was alive in there.'

The driver of the donkey cart could see two men furiously riding towards him. He fervently hoped they would overtake him and let him get on with delivering his load. He was sure he could already sense the stink of the corpse he carried. But the riders pulled up by him and bade him to stop.

'Was this the coffin collected at the Green Dragon?' asked one of the men.

'Who wants to know?' responded the donkey cart driver.

'I'm the landlord of the Green Dragon and I believe the man in this coffin is alive.' With that he jumped down from his horse and started hitting the coffin. He waited to see if there was a response. Nothing.

The landlord turned to the ostler. 'Are you sure you heard the noises?'

'Oh yes sir. I may not have known that I was sleeping on a coffin but I did hear the scratching and the banging. And it all came from under me.'

'Then we must open this coffin. Give me the crowbar.'

The donkey cart driver tried to stop him but he was shoved away.

The crowbar was applied. The lid was lifted.

In the coffin the shrouded body had turned so that the head and feet faced the bottom surface of the coffin and the body was severely contorted as if in a final struggle to make himself heard. He was dead now.

No one knew the four men who brought the coffin. The letter gave no address. The men were never traced.

The old Green Dragon Inn in Axminster stood for another hundred years and was demolished in the early nineteenth century. Locals would tell you that when the stables were empty, you could hear a scratching, thumping and occasionally a moaning. The house was rebuilt in the mid-nineteenth century and is now a fine bed and breakfast. However, the stables are still there, converted to a cottage. Nowadays, no one admits to hearing any rustling noises or moans. But maybe the television is turned up too loud?

16

THE KING OF ENGLAND'S REVENGE: KILMINGTON

'**M**ercia muck!'
  'Wessex weasel!'
  'Northumbria nowt!'

The sun had gone down and the sentries at the Saxon camp stood alert. They hurled abuse at each other, making jokes as they kept warm, listening to the crackle of the fire and attentive to any sound – maybe a broken twig? Tomorrow would be a great battle and who knew if they would survive. But tonight, they would be vigilant to any potential raid by the Vikings from Dublin, with their accursed allies the Celtic men from the north, from Alba and Strathclyde.

Some of them had fought alongside their king, Athelstan, for a long time. They had many memories of the battles on the northern borders and pushing back at the Northmen at York. They had celebrated when the three kingdoms of Mercia (the mucks!)

Wessex (the weasels!) and Northumbria (the nowts!) had come together and Athelstan had been proclaimed King of the English. Each man was still proud of where he came from and suffered the regional loyalties of his comrades.

All of them were loyal to Athelstan and determined to serve their king as best they could. One army. One nation. All Englishmen. Now the Vikings had landed at Axmouth with their allies. As they warmed their hands over the fire, the sentries worried that the battle was close to the heart of their own lands, to the southern coast, to Dumnonia – or, as we know it, Devon. The Vikings wanted to battle in the Saxon homelands, in the hope that distant Northumbria would be given up. But Athelstan, King of the English, would have a plan.

A shadow stood beneath the trees and watched them. Under his cloak was a small lyre. His fingers stroked it nervously. Then he stepped forward, making as much noise as possible.

'Who goes there?' went the call from the youngest sentry.

The shadow laughed and held out his lyre to the light of the fire. 'It is only a minstrel come to play you a tune to soothe your night before battle.' His fingers ran over the lyre strings with a pleasant discordant note.

'Are you an Englishman?' asked the sentry again, his voice a slight quiver. He was aware that his more experienced colleagues were watching him and smiling to themselves.

'I am as much an Englishman as any of you! Let me tell you a story and play you a song.'

'What weapons do you carry?' The sentry was determined to do his task.

'None but my voice and the notes from the lyre.'

The young sentry tried to challenge again but one of his colleagues cuffed him from behind.

'He is what he says he is. A minstrel. Take no notice of him, minstrel, come sit down by us, I have a mind to listen to a song or two.'

And thus Anlaf, King of the Vikings in Dublin, walked into the camp of Athelstan, King of England, to assess the size and placement of his enemy's camp.

A song? A story? A few coins passed to him in tribute and thanks. Anlaf moved around the camp, welcomed as diversion in the long night and thoughts of the next day.

It took a couple of hours but when most of the Saxon soldiers started to bed down, he took his farewell. The coins in his pocket jangled as he walked along. He was now armed with the information he needed to disperse his troops. Most importantly, he had found where Athelstan rested with his earls. He almost smiled at how easy it was and how gullible the Saxons were, these so-called Englishmen.

As he reached the edge of the camp, it came to him that it was dishonourable to walk away with the coins of the men he would slaughter the next day. Under a large oak tree, he knelt down, scooped some earth out, placed the pouch of coins there and covered it over. He stood up and was about to turn in to the wood, when another Saxon sentry caught sight of him. A much older man.

Anlaf now was full of confidence and stepped towards him. 'A song? A story?' The man shook his head and Anlaf stepped back into the shadows and into the night, hurrying as fast as he could back to his camp so that he could send his orders.

The old sentry guard watched as Anlaf disappeared in to the trees. He walked up to the oak tree and scuffed the ground, until the pouch came to light. He bent down and picked it up. Coins! But why would a minstrel bury his night's takings?

A memory stirred, a curtain was drawn back and the old guard remembered.

He went straight to Athelstan's camp and demanded he speak to the king. The earls, protecting the king, tried to send him away, but in all the commotion he was making the king awoke and demanded to know what was afoot.

'Sire,' said the sentry, 'I believe that Anlaf has been here tonight, dressed as a minstrel, and he has taken with him knowledge of all our camp.'

Athelstan had seen the minstrel at a distance in the camp, assumed that he was known to his men and was pleased that his men were being placated and aided.

'How do you know it was Anlaf? How would you know what he looks like?'

'Sire,' sighed the sentry, 'I am an old man and I have survived many battles. But I come from Northumbria and I didn't always fight for you. I saw Anlaf many times when he was young and his father was King of Northumbria. He has a distinctive scar on his cheek.'

'Why did you not raise the alarm when you saw him?' Athelstan was pondering the implications of this news.

The old man paused and then looked Athelstan straight into the eye. 'I have taken an oath of loyalty to his father never to cause harm to him or his family. I will never break my oath. Just as I would never break my oath to you.'

Athelstan looked at the old man in front of him and thought of what he had seen and done. 'I believe you,' he said. 'Tomorrow, when you survive the battle, return to your home and tell them how you have served your king. But for now, go back to your post.' He dismissed the old man.

'Now,' he said, turning to the Saxon earls about him, 'I think we have the advantage after all!'

Anlaf summoned his allies Constantine, the King of Alba, and Owen, the King of Strathclyde, and shared what he had seen. They agreed the plan. Together with the men led by the Viking princes, they would encircle the Saxons' camp and slaughter them while they were unprepared. After the initial rout, Anlaf himself would lead a charge on Athelstan's part of the camp and take him prisoner. The three kings would bring justice to the land. Northumbria would be restored to Anlaf as Daneland and act as a buffer so that the English would no longer threaten the Celtic borders of Strathclyde and Alba.

As the sun came up, Anlaf's men were all in place. He surveyed them standing before him. Anlaf knelt down to the ground, picked up a handful of soil and raised it above his head.

He called to his men: 'By sunset this land will run with the blood of the Englishmen, as they call themselves. And their wealth, their land, their cattle will be ours!'

He called out the traditional battle cry: 'Fee!'

The horde responded, 'Fi!'

He cried again, 'Fo!'

'Fum!' came the reply.

'Bring me the blood of the Englishmen!'

The resounding cheers and whoops made Anlaf smile.

This was his battle to win. He turned and led his men to certain victory.

Anlaf watched as the men covered the ground, listened as he could hear the slaughter begin. He called his men and then surged forward.

Then something caught his attention. Surely this was the tree where he had buried the money pouch. That was just on the edge of the encampment, but where his men were fighting was much further ahead. When he caught up with them, he could see the bloodied bodies on the ground but there was no evidence of the Saxon encampment he had seen the night before. The place where he expected to find Athelstan's resting place was now occupied by an old man, who was already on his knees praying.

'Who are you?' demanded Anlaf. 'Where is Athelstan?'

'I don't know, I don't know!' came the pleading reply. 'I am the Bishop of Sherbourne. God's man. A Christian man. We came but a few hours ago and camped here. I don't know anything. Please don't kill me.'

Anlaf reined in his horse and looked about him, confused. This wasn't the great army that he had walked through the night before.

Then a cry! A shout! From out of the woods and trees came the Saxons he had been seeking. Warned, they had moved their camp in the night. The unfortunate bishop, arriving late, had camped with his men in the wrong place.

Now Anlaf's men were encircled. The tables were turned. And there was much bloodshed.

Lord Tennyson's famous 1876 translation of *The Battle of Brunanburh* tells us:

Athelstan King,

Lord among Earls,

Bracelet-bestower and

Baron of Barons,

He with his Brother,

Edmund Atheling,

Gaining a lifelong

Glory in battle,

Slew with the sword-edge

There by Brunanburh,

Brake the shield-wall,

Hew'd the linden-wood,

Hack'd the battle-shield,

Sons of Edward with hammer'd brands.

Theirs was a greatness

Got from their grand-sires–

Theirs that so often in

Strife with their enemies

Struck for their hoards and their hearths

and their homes.

Mighty warriors on both sides were massacred that day.

Athelstan watched in horror as seven of his faithful earls were torn to pieces defending him.

Anlaf gasped as the prime of Viking blood, five of the princes, bold in battle, were struck down and bled to death. Owen, King of Strathclyde, fell on the field. His body was never found. Anlaf and Constantine, King of Alba, fled back to their ships. The men they left behind fought on, until they realised there was no point, just slaughter.

Then the Norse leader–
Dire was his need of it,
Few were his following–
Fled to his war-ship;
Fleeted his vessel to sea with the king in it,
Saving his life on the fallow flood.
Also the crafty one,
Constantinus,
Crept to his North again,
Hoar-headed hero!

Athelstan surveyed the battlefield.

Many a carcase they left to be carrion,
Many a livid one, many a sallow-skin–
Left for the white-tail'd eagle to tear it and
Left for the horny-nibb'd raven to rend it and
Gave to the garbaging war-hawk to gorge it and
That gray beast, the wolf of the weald.

As hard a man as he was, he did not shirk from vomiting at what he surveyed.

With so many dead and dying, there was nothing left but to bury them where they died. The bodies of high rank of Saxon and Viking were found and brought to Athelstan.

Athelstan sought out the bodies of his faithful seven earls who had died and had them laid on biers covered in cloth. He called them by name, bent to embrace each body and whispered a thanks and farewell to each one. His tears dropped to wash their dead faces. 'These men have served me proud. On this day we have routed the Vikings from our shores, so they know the strength of our nation of Englishmen. Take the bodies of these men and we shall give their souls the highest praise.'

Athelstan ordered their bodies to be sent to the place we know as Axminster and buried there. He gave money and land to Newenham Abbey to enable seven priests to pray for the souls of the seven earls and the many other Saxons that died that day.

He turned to the bodies of the five Viking princes. He kicked the nearest one.

He declared, 'You may have been kings and princes in your own way but here you are no more than scum. You followed a

man who deceived you. You have slaughtered the cream of my earls and for that I can never forgive you. You may follow the Christian God but I deny you a Christian burial. You shall not have the rites given to true believers.'

He turned to the men who would dispose of the bodies. 'Put their hands in manacles so that in the afterlife they will be known as men who did hideous deeds and who followed a false leader. So long as they are manacled, they will never make their way to the Kingdom of God.' Their bodies were sent to a place we know now as Kilmington. There they were buried in graves, their hands manacled together so that in the afterlife they would be known as faithless men.

So many other bodies were buried, unceremoniously. A yew tree was planted so that it would be known as a place of the dead and as a lesson for all.

The battle was fought, so some people say, around Warlake Hill; and on certain nights the ghosts of the five manacled Viking warrior princes rise from their graves, to drink from the lake and rattle their chains as they make their way back to their burial ground. Denied the rituals of the Christian Church, their souls continue to wander the earth, looking for redemption. While they wear their chains there can be no forgiveness.

On the beach at Axmouth, there can be seen the ghost of a warrior searching the beaches. Looking, perhaps, for his ship that has sailed without him, abandoning him to the Saxons.

There is some evidence that Fee, Fie, Fo, Fum was used as a call and response. I used it as a war cry for the Vikings as one of their runes is Fehu, which can mean wealth.

The Billings directory and gazetter of Devonshire of 1857 states that 'Kilmington, originally spelt Kilmenton, which took its name from the great slaughter of the Danes in Athelstan's day, as much to say the place of slain men, for here they were forced to fly over the River Axe and were vanquished.'

The yew tree stood for many years until it fell and was replaced by a stone laid flat in the grass in the graveyard. In 1994, Major General G.M. Elliot wrote: 'To find it enter by the south gate and, where the path swings left to the church porch, turn right and take about 7 paces towards a grave marked by a stone cross.' Alas, I have been unable to find it – but maybe you will!

17

NIGHT-TIME REVELS: SOMEWHERE IN EAST DEVON

I'm not a very good gardener. Oh, I can keep it neat and tidy but I'm of the natural garden school of gardening. Let it grow! That's all right for me, I love sitting in the garden amid a mass of wild flowers and grass as high as it gets. But then my friend asked if she could come and visit. Now she has one of those immaculate gardens and always wins all the prizes in the local Village in Bloom competitions. I was so surprised, I said yes before I realised what that would mean.

Now I confess that she does intimidate me a bit and especially about my gardening skills. I looked around and knew that the garden would need just a bit more than tidying up. I know full well that I shouldn't worry about what other people think but somehow my friend always gets to me. Fortunately my neighbour, Audrey, suggested that her gardener was looking for some extra hours and could help out. I was seriously grateful for that.

On the appointed day it was blustery and the sky was very dark. Not quite raining but promising a storm. The gardener's name was Sharleen and she had come from India. 'It's always much warmer there,' she said.

She got stuck into the gardening and was very meticulous. She found things growing in my garden I didn't even know about. I was writing away and after an hour or so I decided to take a break. She was still working hard and I could see she was going to be there for some time. I offered her a cup of tea and she accepted. We sat in the lounge where I was doing my writing. Politely, she asked what I was doing. I told her: *Devon Ghost Tales*.

She had been about to take a sip of her tea but then did a double take. 'Has Audrey been talking to you?'

I looked at Sharleen and wondered what she meant. 'Well, all that she said was that you were a very good gardener,' I replied.

'That's not what I was thinking,' she whispered.

She drank her tea and then slowly lowered her cup and saucer, placing it on the coffee table in front of her. I had one of those old-fashioned doily things on it and she played with the edge of the embroidered lace for a few moments.

She looked to one side, then back at me. Her lips were moving, as if she was practising what she might say. 'I had something happen to me.'

She stopped. Looked at me again. 'I'm not a crazy woman. But something really happened to me.'

I nodded to her and tried to be reassuring. When you are writing a book like *Devon Ghost Tales*, you do get into some interesting conversations.

'Please tell me,' I reassured her.

'Will you put it into your book?'

I smiled. I had this a lot, too. 'I don't know. It depends on the story. But I like to hear all kinds of story. So tell me anyway.'

I could see my pen and paper on the table and the computer light was flashing. I really should get back to what I was writing but I decided that I had a few minutes to spare. 'Please tell me. I won't write anything if you don't want me to.'

'I need to tell someone,' she said, 'I can't keep carrying this by myself.

'I know that I am working for you as a gardener. I like the work, it makes me relax and it helps me to feel the earth and to see things grow. For my day job, the one that brings me in the money I need, I'm a healthcare assistant. I work in an old people's home; it's here in East Devon.

'I'd been living here in England for some years, working in residential care homes. I like the work and I'm good at it. I trained as a nurse in India, and employers like that kind of experience even if they don't recognise the qualification.

'I had the interview for the job and then flew out to Mumbai to see my family. It was while I was there I got the message that they wanted me to start the day after I got back from my holiday. I wrote and asked for a day's grace but they were very insistent.

'My flight was delayed by two hours and when I got in I took a taxi to the care home straight away. It was eight o'clock at night and one of the care staff answered the door. They weren't expecting me! I was supposed to be living in, so I didn't have any other accommodation arranged. I had nowhere else to go. They rang through to the housekeeper and she was also surprised to see me. I tried to explain that I was due to start work with them the next day and I was living in. She was very grumpy and I supposed she had been dragged away from watching *EastEnders* in order to deal with me. Faced with the contract and copies of the correspondence she conceded that there had been a mistake made.

'"I'll have to put you on the top floor," she said. "They are mainly storage rooms and a spare bedroom. I don't have any other staff rooms at the moment." At that point I didn't care. I was so tired all I wanted to do was get my head down.

'We took the lift up to the fourth floor. As the lift door opened, I could see that this part of the house seemed older than the rest of it. The housekeeper nodded.

'"This used to be an old manor house. All the other floors were renovated but this floor is oddly shaped. The roof slopes on one side and they haven't modernised it yet."

'She stepped out of the lift, took some keys out of her pocket and handed them to me. "Your room is number three. Just up there." She indicated up the hall. There were doors on either side, leading off, and the hall light was already flickering. I was worried it might go soon and leave me in the dark. I wondered if I should ask for a spare bulb but I didn't want to keep her away from *EastEnders* any longer than I needed to.

'She waited until I had staggered out with my suitcase and rucksack and then slipped back into the lift again. "If you come to my office at nine o'clock in the morning, I'll sort out your accommodation properly and tell you what shifts you are on."

'I was surprised that she was just leaving me. "Is the room made up?" I asked. If they weren't expecting me, how would the room be ready? "There are always two beds made up in that room," she said before the lift doors closed.

'I was so tired, I didn't care. I picked up my bags and made my way to the room. It wasn't even locked. I pushed the door open. It did that screeching thing. I shuddered. I gave up and just threw my bags into the room, while I tried to find the light switch. It wasn't one of those white flat things but a brown knobby thing, with a little pivot handle. I pulled it down and the light spluttered on. There were two single beds in the room, a wardrobe and a chest of drawers. There was a lamp by the bed but the shade had seen better days. A wooden chair was next to the door. Sparse is not the word for it. But it was more than some people had in the world, so I was grateful and it would only be for one night.

'I moved my bags and put the bedside light on. The glare caught the flailing threads of the lampshade and I decided to remove it in case it was a fire hazard. There appeared to be clean sheets and a blanket on each bed. My eyes were drooping. I just needed to rest. I turned the main light off. Took my shoes off and then just got into bed. I reached up and turned out the naked bulb.

'I don't know how long I was asleep, but I could feel this hand on my shoulder, shaking me. "Wake, up," they said. "You're in my bed." I cursed the housekeeper for not telling me there was someone sharing the room. I rolled over, trying to get my brain in gear. Everything was still in darkness.

'"I'm sorry," I said, "I didn't know that anyone else was sleeping here."

'"It's my bed. Get out!"

'The voice was getting higher pitched and the hand was rough on my shoulder. I tried to work out who was in the room. It was a female voice, although it seemed to be a bit young for someone working in care home. I could see her against the moonlight.

She seemed shorter than me and I could just see the outline of long hair, with wisps that curl up on themselves.

'The bedside light wouldn't work and all I wanted to do was sleep. So I rolled over to the other side, got out and straight into the other bed. It was very cold and I was shivering. I heard the other woman slide into the warm bed I'd left. I thought that was very strange. I don't know about you but I wouldn't sleep in a bed that a stranger had just left. I'd like at least a change of sheets.

'I tried to get to sleep again but the person in the next bed was tossing and turning. I thought that she might even have been crying. But I just wanted to sleep. When I awoke in the morning, the other bed was already made and no one to be seen.

'I wondered who the other woman was. As I made my way down the stairs I met other members of staff, who just nodded as I passed them and then whispered to each other. The residents were delightful, with one of them letting go of her Zimmer frame, grabbing my hand and asking, "Are you the new girl?"

'I hate being called "girl" – I'm an adult woman – but I let it pass because in comparison to most of them I suppose I was very much younger.

'I made my way to the housekeeper's office – not really sure whether I should be reporting to her or the care home manager. I knocked on her door and waited until she called "Enter". It felt like being back at school.

'"Ah, yes," she said, barely looking up. "I'm sorry about last night but I wasn't expecting you until the sixth of next month, not this. However, I can see that it's a mistake on the care side – they sent me all the wrong dates. They *are* expecting you today and your first shift started an hour ago. So you better go there and get it all sorted out."

'I was flabbergasted at her offhand manner and didn't know how to respond. I almost turned away, when I remembered. "And where am I sleeping?" She paused and this time looked at me. "You'll be all right in that room until next week, won't you? I have nothing else until then."

'"But what about the person I'm sharing with?" I didn't want another night being woken up. She paused again and then seemed to be choosing her words carefully. "I'm sure that won't be a problem. You will be fine. Nothing to worry about. It will be all right." With that, she turned away and picked up her phone. I was obviously dismissed.

'I did not feel at all welcome and was questioning whether I would be staying in the job much longer. But the other care assistants were very helpful and friendly and the care manager put me more at ease.

'"Don't worry about the housekeeper," she said. "This was her family home until they sold it about fifty years ago. It was very nostalgic for her to come back and work here. She can be quirky but she is very good at her job."

'I asked about my room-mate but nobody seemed to know who she was. Some of them said she might be on the housekeeping side and they didn't all know each other. I could find out no more. "It's only for a week," I thought. That night I decided to use the second bed in the room but when I went to unpack, I found that all the wardrobes and drawers were empty.

'"Perhaps she moved out anyway – didn't want to share," I thought. I got into bed and read my book. By the time I turned the light out, no one had arrived to claim the other bed, so I felt more comfortable sleeping there.

'I was awoken by the sounds of what seemed like whispering and then laughter. As though there were children in the room. I wondered at first if someone in the room beneath me had the television up loud but then I heard the distinctive sounds of shoes scudding on the floorboards and a mattress creaking as if someone was bouncing on it.

'"Who's there?" I called out.

'The noises stopped. I heard footsteps crossing the room. Then a shriek. "Someone's in my bed. Someone's in my bed!" The screams crescendoed and then cut off.

'I sat up and struggled with the side lamp. By the time it came on there was nothing to be seen. Nothing that is, apart from the condition of the other bed. The covers were rumpled and there were indentations in the surface as if someone had been bouncing on it in their shoes.

'I was getting annoyed at my anonymous room-mate. Even if she had moved out because of me, it wasn't right that she should treat me like this. I decided to teach her a lesson. I locked the door and then put the chair under the door handle. If she wanted to get back into the room then she would have to wake me up and at least I would get to meet her, rather than let these childish games go on.

'I didn't sleep through the night. I'd been expecting a confrontation and wasn't really sure how I would handle it. I suppose I drifted off at about six o'clock and I must have awoken at about seven. The first thing I noticed was that the chair was back in its usual place and the bed next to me had the covers straightened, with no sign of the foot marks. I was pretty annoyed that somehow she had got into the room and out again without me hearing her. I guessed that the chair under the door handle wasn't as much of a barrier as I thought. I wondered if I should challenge the house-keeper about the identity of my anonymous room-mate. But I didn't want to make a fuss and jeopardise my new job. I got on with my duties, while trying to work out who had been sharing my room. I'd only seen an outline on the first night and heard a voice. But no one I met matched my experience.

'The next day I was on night shift. It was a twelve-hour shift from eight in the evening to eight in the morning. There were three floors and eight rooms a floor. I had to cover the top floor, just below where I was sleeping. After they had supper, some of the residents watched television but the more elderly ones went straight to bed. By the time I came on shift most were asleep and their medication had already been dispensed for the night. My job was to check on them regularly and settle anyone who was disturbed. The registered nurse was available for me to call if they needed more attention.

'I did my hourly round just after midnight. Miss Deegan was still awake. She was lying on her bed and the hall light behind me just caught in her eyes. She raised one hand to me and beck-oned me to her bed. "Are they coming?" she rasped. "Are they coming?" I assumed that she meant her family and I reassured her that they would be there, making a mental note to myself to check her file to see if they were coming. But she became more distressed. "I don't want them to come. They are always so noisy. Don't let them come!" I tried to calm her down by saying that she didn't have to see anyone if she didn't want to. She nodded and gave a sigh of relief. I resolved to check the file.

'In the next room, Mr Fitzhenry was sitting in his armchair in his pyjamas and dressing gown with just the small light on. In front of him on the side table was a Mars bar, some boiled sweets and some other chocolates. I suggested that he should get back into bed but he shook his head and said, "I don't want to miss out on the fun." I asked him what kind of fun but he just put his finger to cover his lips and shushed me. I decided to finish the round and if he was still in his chair I'd get the nurse.

'In the fifth bedroom, Mrs Pickford was fast asleep but had all the lights on. I couldn't see any reason to leave the main light on and the permanent night light was working all right so I turned it off and closed the door quietly.

'In the final bedroom, Mrs Jones was sitting up in bed. Her side light was on and she was stroking the long hair of an old doll. She seemed disappointed when I came into the room. "Do you think she will like this?" she asked, holding up the doll. It had clearly seen better days and looked like it could have been her own one when she was a child. I wondered if she was planning to give it to her grandchild. I knew I needed to read the files a bit more. "Yes," I said, "I'm sure she will love it." Mrs Jones smiled. "I do hope so," she said.

'I checked on Mr Fitzhenry again. He was insistent that he didn't want to go to bed. "They'll be coming soon. Just let me have another half an hour and I'll be in bed then." I smiled at him, thinking the day staff were not going to be too happy with me if I didn't get him to bed soon. They would have a job getting him up. "All right, I'll give you until my next round!" He had such a look of delight on his face – like a small boy waiting for his best friend.

'I went back to my desk station. I looked at the hall light. Bold, modern and very bright in stark contrast to the one on the floor above. I decided to turn off some of the hall lights – perhaps they were disturbing the residents so that they couldn't sleep.

'I pulled out my copy of the local newspaper and started to read. It's always dangerous to read for too long when on night duty. Your eyes just close for a second and then you jerk awake. I thought I could hear someone calling out so I stood up. Then I heard it. Laughter. Children's laughter. It was coming from one of the rooms. That's when Miss Deegan screamed. "Go away, please make them go away!"

'I went straight to her room. As I got there, again I could hear laughter but this time in front of me, on my side of the door, and just for a few seconds I could feel a chill go up my spine and something cold touch my cheek. It was like being thrown into the cold water when your kayak capsizes. I gasped and then turned the handle. There was Miss Deegan, in her bed, knees drawn up under her chin, pulling up the bedclothes with one hand, while batting away something in front of her.

'"Make them go away!"

'I turned on the light. She reached towards me, grasped my arm and then burst into tears. I was holding her as she sobbed, with one ear as to what was happening outside. More laughter out in the corridor and then a deep shout.

'"Wait for me!" It was Mr Fitzhenry.

'I had no idea what was going on. Was this some kind of mass hysteria? I extricated myself from Miss Deegan, promising her I would be back and went into Mr Fitzhenry's room. He was on his knees on the bed, bouncing up and down. The chocolate and boiled sweets had gone from the side table but the brown smear across his face suggested that he had eaten at least some of it. As I came into the room he called out, "Stop – don't leave me."

'Standing in the doorway, I heard that laughter and felt a sensation of cold then a prickling up and down my arms as if icy fingers were touching me. Mr Fitzhenry stopped bouncing and looked at me.

'"You scared them off! It's not fair. We were having such fun."

'A scream cut through the night. Mrs Pickford. Now I knew why she left the light on. I was at the other end of the hall from my station – should I go back and summon the nurse, or do what I could? She screamed again.

'"I'm coming!" I called. But was I reassuring her, or giving a warning to something else?

'I opened her door. By the nightlight I could see Mrs Pickford was lying on the bed, arms by her side, eyes squeezed shut.

'"Leave me alone. Please don't touch me."

'I turned on the light as I called out her name. Her eyes flew open.

'"You! You turned the lights off. You put me through this hell just to save a few pennies on the meter. Damn you!"

'I was astonished at her tone and didn't know what to say.

Behind me there was more laughter coming from the other side of the corridor. I just shook my head at Mrs Pickford, left the light on and the door open, then went to Mrs Jones's room. I tried the door handle but the door wouldn't open. Inside I could hear Mrs Jones laugh and say, "I'm so glad you like it. You can keep it."

'I banged on the door. "Mrs Jones! Are you all right? Can you open the door?"

'"Go away," she replied, "I'm having fun with my friends."

'Now I knew I need help. I went to the desk and used the intercom to get the nurse who was downstairs. I told her some of the patients were disturbed and asked that she come up as soon as possible. I went to the middle of the hallway. Four patients sleeping and four patients agitated. "Enough!" I called out. "Enough of this!"

'Then all the lights in the hall and the rooms went out. The glimmering green of the emergency lights came on. The lift whirred and the doors opened, its bright internal light shone on me. It was the housekeeper. "What's going on here?" she cried. I stuttered and tried to explain but she cut across me. "How are the residents?" I was confused and wondered where the nurse was. She was supposed to be on her way. I just responded to the question and led her around the rooms.

'All the doors opened. All of them were asleep. Miss Deegan had the sheet over her head and snored gently. Mr Fitzhenry was back in his bed, although with the telltale smear of chocolate still on his cheek. Mrs Pickford had left the main light on but was fast asleep. The other residents remained undisturbed. As we came to Mrs Jones's room, I grew apprehensive. Would the door still be locked? But no, it opened easily. The lights were out. She was snoring loudly. The doll was nowhere to be seen. I shook my head. I couldn't make any sense of it.

'The housekeeper turned to me. "I want you to go to your room now, pack all your bags and take them to my office. I'll stay here with the residents."

'I was stunned. Was she sacking me? Did she have the authority to do that?

'"It's all right," she said. Her tone softened. "I should never have put you in that room. When you come off shift in the morning, you can stay in my flat with me until I make other arrangements for you to live here."

'At that point I was too shocked by events to do anything more than as I was told. I turned away and as I walked back to the lift she called out, "Did you see them?"

'I turned back. "Did I see who?"

'She hesitated. "My brother and sister. They died from 'flu in this house fifty years ago. Yours was the room my sister and I shared. He was about five and she was ten. Quite tall for her age, with long dark curly hair. I don't really remember them, I was only aged three."

'"No," I said, "I didn't see anybody."

'I moved my stuff and finished my shift. The next day, before I had breakfast, I rang the agency I'd worked for before, and then handed in my notice. I walked away from that care home that day and have never been back.'

Sharleen finished telling her story and then looked at me, tilting her head on one side. My tea was cold; I hadn't finished drinking it. She put down her cup and stood up.

'Anyway, I'd better get back to pruning your borders. You can use the story but don't say where the care home is. The residents have enough to contend with, without someone else coming in and disturbing them.'

I wasn't sure which residents she meant. The living or the dead.

This was the story that was told to me. Some of the names and details have been changed to reflect Sharleen's request that the care home should not be identified. However, the description of the events that occurred is as she told me.

NOTES ON SOURCES

Full references to all works cited may be found in the Bibliography

1. The Rag Doll: The Prospect Inn, Exeter
I. Addicoat, *Haunted Devon*, p. 46.
R. Matthews, *Haunted Places of Devon*, p. 35.
www.exetermemories.co.uk/em/_pubs/prospect.php

2. The Pencil: Exmouth to Exeter
C. Hole, *Haunted England*.
H. Spicer, *Strange Things Among Us*.
P. White, *Classic Devon Ghost Stories*, p. 8.
R. Whitlock, *The Folklore of Devon*, p. 59.
The original version is in Spicer, and all the other sources draw on it.

3. A Father's Sins: Princesshay, Exeter
There are two versions of this ghost story in circulation. The first is that it is Queen
 Henrietta Maria, wife of Charles I, with her daughter. The second is that it is her
 daughter, Princess Henrietta, grown as a woman with her companion, who was a
 dwarf.
I. Addicoat, *Haunted Devon*, p. 42.
T. Brown, *Devon Ghosts*, p. 40.
'A Princess is Born', http://www.exetermemories.co.uk/em/civilwar.php#princess
'Bedford Circus and Bedford Street', www.exetermemories.co.uk/em/_streets/bedfordstreet.php
'Queen Henrietta Maria, 1609–69', bcw-project.org/biography/henrietta-maria
'The History of Bedford House', demolition-exeter.blogspot.co.uk/2010/09/bed-
 ford-house-and-dominican-friary.html

4. This Foul Priest: Lapford
T. Brown, *Devon Ghosts*, pp. 68–70.
R. Matthews, *Haunted Places of Devon*, p. 93.
R.E. St Leger-Gordon, *Witchcraft and Folklore of Devon*, p. 53.
V.D. Sharman, *Folk Tales of Devon*, pp. 74–5.

H.P. Whitcombe, *Bygone Days in Devon and Cornwall*, pp. 125–6.

R. Whitlock, *The Folklore of Devon*, p. 56.

5. The Wrecker's Legacy: Ilfracombe

I. Addicoat, *Haunted Devon*, p. 30.

T. Brown, *Devon Ghosts*, p. 135.

'Chambercombe Manor', en.wikipedia.org/wiki/Chambercombe_Manor.

'The Hidden Body', Ilfracombe, ancestry.co.uk/boards/surnames.oatway/4/
    mb.ashx?pnt=1

6. A Dead Man's Request: Spreyton

T. Brown, *Devon Ghosts*, pp. 75–8.

S.B. Gould, *Devonshire Characters and Strange Events*, https://en.wikisource.org/wiki/
    Devonshire_Characters_and_Strange_Events

A. Lang, *Book of Dreams and Ghosts*, http://www.gutenberg.org/ebooks/12621

They are all based on a document from 1683 and their contents are more or less identical.

7. The Legend of Benjamin Geare: Okehampton

T. Brown, *Devon Ghosts*, pp. 139–40.

M. Dacre, *Devonshire Folk Tales*, pp. 70–3.

P. White, *Classic Devon Ghost Stories*, p. 30.

R. Whitlock, *The Folklore of Devon*, pp. 54–5.

There are many variants of the legend of Benji Geare, some with details that do not
    appear in this version!

8. The Silver Ink Pot: Hayne Manor, Stowford

T. Brown, *Devon Ghosts*, p. 81.

J. Chard, *Devon Stories of the Supernatural*.

P. Underwood, *Ghosts of Devon*, pp. 87–9.

9. The Footpad's Gamble: Down House, Tavistock

The earliest reference to this story is in Mrs Bray, *The Borders of the Tamar and the
    Tavy*, vol. II, p. 129, www.sacred-texts.com/neu/eng/efft/efft58.htm. It mainly
    consists of the scene at the end of the confrontation between the ghost and
    the mother and father. All other references draw on this source, and don't add
    anything to the story. In my version I have developed the backstory of the ghost,
    and how he came to be there.

10. Lovers by the Gravestone: Killworthy House, Tavistock

P. Underwood, *Ghosts of Devon*, pp. 90–2.

There is an unsigned typed manuscript at the Glanville tomb, Tavistock parish church.

11. Two Sisters: Berry Pomeroy

T. Brown, *Devon Ghosts*, pp. 33–4.

D. Seymour, *The Ghosts of Berry Pomeroy Castle*.

P. Underwood, *Ghosts of Devon*.
Several books held no more than a few words of the jealousy of the sisters, so I merely give three key references.

12. The Spanish Lady Who Pretended to be a Boy: Torre Abbey, Torquay

M. Rhodes, *Devon's Torre Abbey: Faith, Politics and Grand Design*.

C. Field, 'Trail Of The Spanish Armada Battlefield Britain', /www.culture24.org.uk/history-and-heritage/military-history/tra22821

Torbay Council Library Services, 'The Spanish Armada Maritime History', www.torbay.gov.uk/media/1844/maritimehistory.pdf

R. Matthews, 'The Spanish Armada abandons the galleon *Nuestra Senora del Rosario*', thehistorymanatlarge.blogspot.co.uk/2012/03/spanish-armada-abandons-galleon-nuestra.html?m=1

13. A Fathers Love : Dartmouth

Whitlock, R. 1977 *The Folklore of Devon* p 53
Underwood, P. 2003 *Ghosts of Devon* p 48-50

14. To Fulfil the Abbot's Desire : Lidwell Chapel , Haldon Hill

Chard, J. 2003 Devon, *Stories of the Supernatural* pp58-60
Underwood, P. 2003 *Ghosts of Devon* p70

Lidwell Chapel and The Monk of Haldon

keatsghost.wordpress.com/connections/places/lidwell-chapel-and-the-monk-of-haldon/

15. Following the Old Corpse Road: Axminster

Styles, C. 1988 *"Weaving a Yarn" in Heritage : The British Review* no 21 p 42- 44

16. The King of England's Revenge: Kilmington

Baring- Gould. S. 1899 *Book of the West* p 45-8
Elliot. Maj Gen G.M. 1969, reprinted 1994, *A brief History of Kilmington*
Tarling, J.F. 2016 *Axminster's minster: a guide to the Church with back ground history*
Tennyson 1876 Translation of The Battle of Brunanburh
Whitlock, R. 1977 *The Folklore of Devon* p 105
Wood, A. 2013 *Military Ghosts*

The site for the Battle of Brunamburh is disputed, with most scholars saying it is up north. However, there is some circumstantial evidence that it was on Warlake Hill near Axminster and Kilmington. The local legends are quite specific about where the seven Saxon earls and the five manacled Viking princes are buried, and where the latter are supposed to haunt.

17. Night-time Revels: Somewhere in East Devon

This was a story told to me.

BIBLIOGRAPHY

Addicoat, I., *Haunted Devon* (Tempus, 2006)

Barber, S. and C. *Dark and Dastardly Dartmoor* (Obelisk Publications, 1995)

Baring-Gould. S., *Book of the West* (1899)

Baring-Gould, S., *Devonshire Characters and Strange Events* (1908),
    https://en.wikisource.org/wiki/Devonshire_Characters_and_Strange_Events

Brown, T., 'Tales of a Dartmoor Village', *West Country Folklore*, no. 7 (1973)

Brown, T., *Devon Ghosts* (Jarrold, 1982)

Caine, M. and A. Gorton, *Devon's Haunted Houses* (Orchard, 2015)

Chard, J., *Devon, Stories of the Supernatural* (Countryside Books, 2003)

Dacre, M., *Devonshire Folk Tales* (History Press, 2010)

Elliot, Maj. Gen. G.M., *A Brief History of Kilmington* (1969, reprinted 1994)

Farquharson-Coe, A., *Devon's Folklore and Legends* (James Pike, 1974)

Gardner, S., *Haunted Exeter* (History Press, 2011)

Garnett, W., *Horrors and Hauntings in Devon* (Tabb House, 1989)

Greathead, H., *Spooky Devon* (Hometown World, 2011)

Hole, C., *Haunted England* (1940)

Hynes, K., *Haunted Dartmoor* (History Press, 2014)

Lang, A., *Book of Dreams and Ghosts* (1899)

Mann, B., *The Ghosts of Totnes* (Obelisk Publications, 1993)

Matthews, R., *Haunted Places of Devon* (Countryside Books, 2004)

Norris, S., *Tales of Old Devon* (Countryside Books, 1991)

Pegg, J., *After Dark on Dartmoor* (John Pegg, 1985)

Phipps, W.J.H., *Devon's Worthies* (A. Wheaton & Co., 1903)

Rhodes, M., *Devon's Torre Abbey* (History Press, 2015)

Seymour, D., *The Ghosts of Berry Pomeroy Castle* (Obelisk Publications, 1994)

Sharman, V.D., *Folk Tales of Devon* (Thomas Nelson & Sons, 1952)

Spicer, H., *Strange Things Among Us* (1863)

St Leger-Gordon, R.E., *Witchcraft and Folklore of Devon* (Bell Publishing Co., 1965)

Talbot, J.F., *Axminster's Minster: A Guide to the Church with Background History* (2016)

Torbay Library Maritime History, *The Spanish Armada* (Devon Local Studies, 2017)

Turner, J., *Ghosts in the South West* (David and Charles, 1973)

Underwood, P., *Ghosts of Devon* (Bossiney Books, 2003)

White, P., *Classic Devon Ghost Stories* (Tor Mark Press, 1996)

Whitcombe, H.P., *Bygone Days in Devon and Cornwall* (1874)

Whitlock, R., *The Folklore of Devon* (B.T. Batsford Ltd, 1977)

Wood, A., *Military Ghosts* (Amberley, 2013)